PRAISE FOR *DARK ROAD*

'*Dark Road* establishes Rankin as the fresh new voice of Scottish theatre. With Thomson, he has produced an unpretentious, honest evening's entertainment'

Evening News

'Excellent entertainment indeed' *Financial Times*

'*Dark Road* is a gripping and chilling piece of psychological drama, paced expertly by its creators and brought to life both by an accomplished cast and striking design'

Edinburgh Spotlight

'Utterly gripping, gritty and great entertainment, this is a welcome and long overdue addition to the theatrical thriller genre' *Public Reviews*

'A creepily believable mixture of anger and geniality'

Guardian

'A great cast, a stunningly ambitious rotating pedestal of sets designed by Francis O'Connor and a whodunit reveal which is typically Rankin' *Independent*

'The psychological cat and mouse game . . . is top-notch prime time stuff' *Herald*

'*Dark Road* teeters at that crossroads of modern era and golden age, warning us that for all the material world changes, human nature remains the same' *TV Bomb*

By Ian Rankin

The Inspector Rebus series

Knots and Crosses
Hide and Seek
Tooth and Nail
Strip Jack
The Black Book
Mortal Causes
Let It Bleed
Black and Blue
The Hanging Garden
Death Is Not the End (*novella*)
Dead Souls
Set in Darkness
The Falls
Resurrection Men
A Question of Blood
Fleshmarket Close
The Naming of the Dead
Exit Music
Standing in
Another Man's Grave
Saints of the Shadow Bible

The Inspector Fox series

The Complaints
The Impossible Dead

Other novels

The Flood
Watchman
Westwind
Doors Open

Writing as Jack Harvey

Witch Hunt
Bleeding Hearts
Blood Hunt

Short stories

A Good Hanging and
Other Stories
Beggars Banquet
The Beat Goes On:
The Complete Rebus Stories

Non-fiction

Rebus's Scotland

Omnibus editions

Rebus: The Early Years
(Knots and Crosses, Hide and
Seek, Tooth and Nail)
Rebus: The St Leonard's Years
(Strip Jack, The Black Book,
Mortal Causes)
Rebus: The Lost Years
(Let It Bleed, Black and Blue,
The Hanging Garden)
Rebus: Capital Crimes
(Dead Souls, Set in
Darkness, The Fall)

Stage Play with Mark Thomson

Dark Road

All Ian Rankin's titles are available on audio.
Also available: *Jackie Leven Said* by Ian Rankin and Jackie Leven.

Ian Rankin is the internationally bestselling author of the Inspector Rebus and Detective Malcolm Fox novels, as well as a string of standalone thrillers. His books have been translated into thirty-six languages and are bestsellers on several continents. Ian is the recipient of four CWA Dagger Awards and in 2004 won America's celebrated Edgar Award. He is also the recipient of honorary degrees from the universities of Abertay, St Andrews, Hull and Edinburgh, and received the OBE for services to literature. Find out more at www.ianrankin.net

Mark Thomson has been the Artistic Director of the Royal Lyceum Theatre in Edinburgh since 2003. Before that he was the Artistic Director of the Brunton Theatre, during which time he directed twenty productions, of which nine were world premieres. In the ten years Mark has been Artistic Director of the Lyceum there have been over twenty world premieres, including his collaboration with Ian.

IAN RANKIN
MARK THOMSON
DARK ROAD

An Orion paperback

First published in Great Britain in 2014
by Orion Books
This paperback edition published in 2015
by Orion Books,
an imprint of The Orion Publishing Group Ltd,
Carmelite House, 50 Victoria Embankment,
London EC4Y 0DZ

An Hachette UK company

2 4 6 8 10 9 7 5 3 1

A CIP catalogue record for this book
is available from the British Library.

ISBN 978-1-4091-5264-4

Printed and bound in Great Britain by
Clays Ltd, St Ives plc

The Orion Publishing Group's policy is to use papers that
are natural, renewable and recyclable products and
made from wood grown in sustainable forests. The logging
and manufacturing processes are expected to conform to
the environmental regulations of the country of origin.

www.orionbooks.co.uk

DARK ROAD: A JOURNEY

As far as I remember, it started almost as a dare.

I've known Mark Thomson for years. He's a playwright and director as well as being Artistic Director of Edinburgh's Lyceum Theatre. There's a café near the theatre where we would rendezvous now and then for coffee and conversation. It was during one of these that we got talking about the popularity of crime. From the bestseller lists to our TV screens – fictional cops seem to be everywhere. But not on the contemporary stage.

'Is that because it can't be done?' Mark asked, throwing down the challenge. 'Why don't we find out?'

So we began work – tentatively – on a story that would become a script, and a script that would end up with a cast attached and the Lyceum booked for three weeks between September and October 2013.

I was very lucky to have Mark as a writing partner. Never having written for the stage before, there were obvious pitfalls I wasn't aware of at first. The cast couldn't be too unwieldy. Sudden shifts of scene or costume were problematic. Too many complicated props or effects and we'd be asking for trouble. Fortunately, Mark steered a clear course between these obstacles, and persuaded set designer Francis O'Connor to come up with a revolving stage that would speed up the action. We knew we wanted to put on a breathless thriller, one that would keep the audience on the edge of their seats. Francis helped make this possible.

Each day for me was full of fascinating new insights. I remember walking into the rehearsal studio and seeing architectural plans pinned to the wall, representing the revolving stage. Then a maquette of the same arrived. Actors were fitted for costumes. A table of props stood ready. Lighting designer Malcolm Rippeth arrived, as did composer Philip Pinsky. Assistant Director Jo Rush was by Mark's side throughout, as was Stage Manager Dan Travis – marking any changes to the script and timing each scene to the absolute second.

Then there were the actors. We knew we were asking a lot of Maureen Beattie – she appears in almost every scene. At the first and second read-throughs, there were questions to be answered as the cast started to get inside the heads of their characters. This process intensified once proper rehearsals got under way, and the complex choreography of each scene started to come alive, the actors adding nuance and texture. The main cast of eight began to gel, finding moments of humour, tension and tenderness in the script, so that the words began to live. It was a particular pleasure for me to meet Ron Donachie (Black Fergus in the play). Ron has

played Rebus several times in BBC radio productions
of my books. Then there was another face I recognised
– Philip Whitchurch. Eventually it dawned on me –
Phil had played a gangster in the TV adaptation of my
novel *Doors Open*. A quality cast from top to bottom,
hand-picked by Mark Thomson and ready for whatever
challenges the production might throw at them.

I attended these rehearsals as often as I could, though
the process by now belonged to the cast and crew rather
than the writer. I was away on a book tour, however,
when the production moved from the Lyceum's rehearsal
studio across the street into the theatre proper. When
I did finally manage a visit, I was overwhelmed once
more. The set really was a thing of wonder, and the
lights, music and visual effects seemed perfect. With the
actors finally in their costumes, we could now see what
the play would look like to an audience. Not that it was
quite the finished article. After the first preview, Mark
made a couple of tough but worthwhile decisions – one
scene got the chop, and a tweak to the finale lessened
the body count ever so slightly.

The result, on opening night, was a spine-tingling
psychological thriller that kept the audience guessing,
had them laughing out loud a few times (at the right
places, thankfully), and made them jump and gasp a few
times, too.

Mark and I had started out wanting to put a
contemporary cop drama on stage, one set in the
Edinburgh of the here and now, and a play that would
prove popular, maybe enticing people away from their

TVs and sofas for a night so we could show them what the theatre can do.

We're delighted that so many people took the journey with us down this particular dark road. Just remember: that light in the distance may not be what you think . . .

Ian Rankin

DARK ROAD

CHARACTERS

Chief Superintendent Isobel McArthur   late forties, Scottish.
Former Chief Constable

Alexandra McArthur   twenty-one, Scottish

Alfred Chalmers   mid–late sixties

Detective Superintendent Frank Bowman   about fifty

Chief Constable Fergus McLintock (Black Fergus)
retired, about seventy, Scottish

Judith   a young female nurse in secure hospital, late twenties

Janice   a young female constable, early–mid twenties

Drew   a young male constable, mid–late twenties

Young Man   about twenty

Sarah McElhenney

Young Male Nurse

Act One

SCENE ONE

Dark. ISOBEL MCARTHUR's sitting room. Homely. Not ultra-modern. Not old-fashioned. Practical, but not furnished without thought and care. Sounds of sex infiltrate.

In front of the sofa a figure or shape of a person appears to be emerging from the floor. Lights crack out. Shouting, and ISOBEL revealed leaping off chair or sofa where she has been asleep. She stands panting. Very slowly and uncertainly she recovers, reflects, looks behind her. She is fully dressed in police uniform.

ALEXANDRA comes through. She is dressed in her nightwear.

ALEXANDRA   Mum? Mum? You OK?

ISOBEL   What?

ALEXANDRA   You OK?

ISOBEL   Yes?

ALEXANDRA   You sure?

ISOBEL   Yes. What time is it?

ALEXANDRA   Late.

ISOBEL   How late?

ALEXANDRA   Late-late.

ISOBEL   Right.

ALEXANDRA   Need anything?

ISOBEL   No, no, I'm fine. It's my thirtieth tomorrow,
            you know.

ALEXANDRA   Mum, you are young for your age but—

ISOBEL   In the force. Done my thirty. Means I can
            retire.

ALEXANDRA   Are you going to?

ISOBEL   Not tomorrow.

ALEXANDRA   Good.

ISOBEL   Is it?

ALEXANDRA   I don't know. Is it? *(Beat)* Go to bed. Maybe
            take your uniform off first.

ISOBEL   Good idea. Good night.

ALEXANDRA   *(Leaving)* You sure you're—

ISOBEL   Yes, yes, love you.

*ALEXANDRA exits. ISOBEL sits down. She opens a laptop
and ruffles a stack of A4 printed pages. The sound of
lovemaking again from the next room.*

SCENE TWO

ISOBEL is in her office. There is the sound of people offstage, laughter, talk. It is ISOBEL's thirtieth. She has a drink in her hand. It's a bare office with some A4 achievement-type things. On one wall there is a board with a mixture of people and cases that she hasn't solved. She is glad to be away from the others. She bursts a balloon with a letter-opener. She puts on the Stone Roses' 'Fool's Gold' and looks out the window. FRANK enters.

FRANK   Thirty years in the force and still no fucking taste.

ISOBEL   Where were you?

FRANK   Sorry, got held up. Miss me?

ISOBEL   I told you I wanted you to be there.

FRANK   That might be the most sentimental thing you have ever said to me.

ISOBEL   Piss off.

FRANK   That's my girl.

ISOBEL   Show some respect for your chief superintendent.

FRANK   All right, boss. You got a drink in here?

ISOBEL   Sorry, only coffee.

FRANK   Of course.

ISOBEL   Know me. Party girl.

FRANK   Was a time.

ISOBEL   Long ago, Frank.

FRANK   Past doesn't just go; s'like carbon – it dates
you.

ISOBEL   Regular enemas do it for me – try it, Frank,
you might be less full of shit.

FRANK   That's my girl.

ISOBEL   Yeah, well.

FRANK   Look who the cat dragged in.

He opens the door. FERGUS enters.

ISOBEL   Fergus!

FERGUS   Yes.

ISOBEL   I'm . . . I'm . . .

FERGUS   And I thought I was the only one old enough
to keep forgetting my name.

ISOBEL   I'm so chuffed you're—

FERGUS   Of course I'd be here.

ISOBEL   That's great.

FERGUS   Can I sit down?

ISOBEL   Of course, just—

FERGUS   Yes, I know how to sit and can still spot a chair
          in a confined space: the wheels creak and clank
          but still turn.

FRANK   What do you think, Fergus?

FERGUS   She looks a million.

FRANK   But the grey?

ISOBEL   Thanks, Frank.

FERGUS   Tough, well-earned and a little bit sexy.

FRANK   Careful, can't say that nowadays.

ISOBEL   Yes he can. What are you doing? Not seen you
          for maybe three years.

FERGUS   I garden, I stalk my grandchildren and try
          and hammer the order and respect into them
          that their empowering, 'you're the centre of
          the universe' parents have failed to do. I wear
          out the hall rug with endless petty trips to the
          kitchen for tea, put things in the bin, tidy up,
          and then there's the increasing trips to the
          bathroom – hard to believe that night-time can
          bring on so much urine with so little drinking.
          So—

ISOBEL   That's an awful lot of information, Fergus.

FERGUS   So my point is, young Isobel—

ISOBEL   That now I've done my thirty and am able to get my pension, it's not all it's cracked up to be out there?

FRANK   She's sharp.

FERGUS   Course she's sharp. She's also a woman, and it's tough here.

ISOBEL   Now, Fergus, that is outright—

FERGUS   I don't care. I'm bloody fond of you and I'll say what I want – I'm sixty-eight and I don't give a shit. One of the benefits. Probably the only benefit.

FRANK   How's your sex life?

FERGUS   *(Glares)* My wife's in a wheelchair.

FRANK   Not all the time.

FERGUS   You've always been a wee bit sick, Frank, haven't you?

FRANK   *(Stands next to ISOBEL)* We are what God and Black Fergus made us. We are your spawn, Black Fergus. We are beautiful, sharp, going grey and sick. And we're yours.

They all laugh.

ISOBEL   Seven years out. You're proof there's life after being a cop. You're looking good.

FERGUS   No, I'm not. Did it bother you not getting
          the top job?

ISOBEL   Didn't get it – over.

FRANK   Still Queen of Police in Edinburgh!

ISOBEL   Yeah.

FERGUS   How's the wee one?

ISOBEL   She's twenty-one.

FERGUS   No she's not.

ISOBEL   She is. Final year at uni.

FERGUS   What's she doing there?

ISOBEL   Film and TV. Doing her final project. Wants
          to be Spielberg. Or a kind of documentary
          Spielberg.

FRANK   In the DNA: search for truth.

ISOBEL   Seeing you . . . You were a great boss, Fergus.
          I have everything to thank you for.

FERGUS   What am I supposed to do with that?

FRANK   Stick it up your jacksie and enjoy.

FERGUS   Listen, we're here to fix the shit when it hits
          the people. *(Beat)* For a wee moment there I
          actually forgot. Was still here, you know, doing
          it. Hang in there.

FRANK   Will do, sir.

FERGUS   I know you will. You've nothing else to do or live for.

FRANK   Cracker. Thanks.

ISOBEL   So much paperwork before I can get at any bad guys . . .

FRANK   Hey – be a chief super and say hello to a big desk of paperwork between you and being a cop.

ISOBEL   Broken record. I'm still a cop, Frank.

FRANK   I do it every day and I can touch it.

ISOBEL   I touch it.

FRANK   Course you do. It's under that paperweight.

ISOBEL   Don't start your real-police shit again. That really why you stayed a detective, so you could still feel the street, Frank?

FRANK   That's why.

ISOBEL   Sure.

FRANK   Absolutely.

ISOBEL   Whatever, I'm still doing it.

FRANK   Really, who with?

ISOBEL   That's crass.

FRANK   That's me. Still got the dirt and mess of the street on my shoes and in my mouth.

ISOBEL   Get a mouthwash and a shoe shine and do us
         all a—

FERGUS   Just like old times.

ISOBEL   I was the first female chief constable in
         Scotland. If I want to retire and go on
         supporting Alexandra, I thought I might write
         a book.

FRANK   What about?

ISOBEL   About me?

FRANK laughs.

ISOBEL   Thanks for that encouragement, Frank.

FRANK   Sorry, I didn't mean to . . . No, well I did. You're
         a cop, not a writer!

ISOBEL   Thought I wasn't a cop?

FRANK   Who'll buy it?

ISOBEL   It's not uninteresting, my job.

FRANK   Course not, but where's the headline? I just
         don't know if 'Scotland's First Female Chief
         Constable' is going to put you on the
         bestseller list.

ISOBEL   No, but Alfred Chalmers might.

Beat.

ISOBEL It's just a thought.

FRANK That's a bad thought.

ISOBEL Maybe.

FRANK That's a bad, bad thought. You put that
thought out your head.

ISOBEL I don't know how much longer I can keep going
at this.

FRANK Not good enough.

ISOBEL It was twenty-five years—

FERGUS —ago this October.

FRANK You've really thought this out. Silver jubilee
of his arrest. Fergus, you say something.

ISOBEL It's a long time ago.

FRANK So why drag him back up? Why drag those
young women's bodies back up? Have you told
their mothers?

ISOBEL You're the first people I've told because I know
it's your story too.

FRANK It's not a fucking story, Isobel, it was a
real-life nightmare and it was yesterday,
I mean yesterday.

FERGUS Have you spoken to him?

Beat.

FRANK   For fuck's sake, Isobel, have you been speaking
to that piece of—

ISOBEL   Not yet.

FRANK   Not yet?

ISOBEL   Not yet.

FRANK paces.

FERGUS   Is there something else, Isobel?

ISOBEL   What do you mean?

FERGUS   The book. The why.

ISOBEL   *(Beat)* I've always had . . . It unnerves me why
I am so uncomfortable with his conviction
twenty-five years on.

FRANK   Oh Jesus Christ.

FERGUS   Not the Lord, Frank.

FRANK   Sorry, Fergus.

ISOBEL   Why does it still bother me? Why can't I
file it?

FERGUS   When we were searching for each one of those
girls' bodies, placed in Chalmers' careful
pattern, pulling legs out of trees, scraping
heads out of rusting oil cans and reading
'It's in the stars' scrawled in blood on their
bellies, the cryptic clue that would lead to the

next part of the human jigsaw; and when we saw that black ugly tar and diamanté jewels where their young shining eyes once had been: well, Isobel, we became participants in his foul quest. He led and we had to dance, or we didn't win. So if then, now, here, you might harbour some doubt *(He physically winces)* about guilt, whether it be his or even your own, like a rattle, loose and unfixed at the back of your head, then distrust it, because it's *his* pattern that makes it.

FRANK   Too right. What he said.

ISOBEL   *(To FRANK)* You're OK about it?

FRANK   Am I OK about him being locked up? You bet your fucking granny's life I'm OK about it.

ISOBEL   We only got him on the fourth – we didn't prove the first three.

FRANK   So what?

ISOBEL   You think that's satisfactory?

FRANK   It was twenty-five years ago.

ISOBEL   That doesn't make it right.

FRANK   It doesn't make it wrong. We got the guy.

ISOBEL   Did we?

FRANK   Please tell me this is a momentary and
             irrational burst of conscience. Or a moment
             of greed to sell your book.

ISOBEL   I don't know. I'm in the middle of it.

FRANK   Get out of the middle of it. Or you put us there
             too. You want that, Isobel? I don't want to
             be there. And neither does Fergus. We don't
             deserve it. You keep your eye on your job, do
             the paperwork, we stop the bad guys hurting
             and stealing and fucking up the good guys, or
             the OK-ish guys, or even the not so bad guys,
             and that's good, that's great, and it doesn't
             work perfectly but it's good. What you're doing,
             it's nothing. It's black. Isn't it, Black Fergus?
             Ask him? Isn't it? Oh fuck.

FRANK exits.

ISOBEL   I don't want to hurt you, Fergus. I've put in
             a request to see him. He might not agree
             anyway. Fergus, Chalmers was put away
             because of eighties forensic evidence that was
             creaky back then on the fourth victim. Nothing
             on the three other girls. He never cracked once.
             I'm not saying he didn't do it, he probably did,
             but . . .

FERGUS gets up with difficulty and in some pain.

FERGUS   The hunch of a police officer has become a playful element of fictional crime-solving. But all this paper piled up neatly, filed and stored, hasn't the weight of a copper's hunch. And I tell you, Isobel, the ugliness of that man, the deep, deep ugliness, was the nearest to pestilence I ever encountered. I know he did it, did all of them. You don't need a wedding ring to know you're loved, Isobel. Don't dirty yourself. Don't bring those girls up again. It won't clear it up. Sorry. Don't do it. Sorry.

FERGUS exits. ISOBEL walks to the door and calls through.

ISOBEL   Drew?

DREW   Ma'am?

ISOBEL   Come here a minute.

DREW enters, a bit worse for wear.

ISOBEL   Drew, can you do me a favour?

DREW   Anything, ma'am, especially today.

ISOBEL   Thank you. I'd like you to arrange to get all the files on a closed case sent over.

DREW   OK.

ISOBEL   *(Writing)* Details here.

DREW   Was that Black Fergus just here?

ISOBEL   Yes, that was him.

DREW   Man's a legend.

ISOBEL   Yes, he is. Here.

She hands him the piece of paper. He looks at it and looks at her. She nods.

ISOBEL   Make sure you get everything. The cassettes. Everything.

DREW   Cassettes? Oh yeah. Any reason?

Beat. DREW starts to go.

ISOBEL   Drew, I'd appreciate it if you kept this to yourself. Saves any silly questions. You know, like the one you just asked.

DREW   Gotcha, ma'am.

ISOBEL   And Drew, I'm very glad you won Tail on the Donkey.

DREW   Me too. It was a good moment for me.

ISOBEL   More to come, I'm sure.

DREW   I hope so.

DREW exits. ISOBEL phones on her mobile.

ISOBEL   Hello. *(Beat)* It's Chief Superintendent
          Isobel McArthur here. Yes, I e-mailed you
          about Alfred Chalmers. Have you had any
          response from him? *(Beat)* Yes, I'm sure he was
          surprised. *(Beat)* No, it's not an official request
          and really I'm . . . well, it's not that I definitely
          want to see him. I wanted to be clear on his
          position. *(Beat)* He's considering it. Right.
          Right. *(Beat)* No, there's no developments, just
          . . . let me know. Thanks. *(Beat)* Thank you.
          Goodbye.

A screech of someone from the party next door.

SCENE THREE

ALEXANDRA at home on the phone, in the middle of a conversation.

ALEXANDRA   Yes. *(Beat)* Yes, that's right. *(Beat)* I'm not fearless; I just want what I do to make a difference, and the more we talk, the more I think we could really do something here. I mean, it's complicated, and people are going to be uncomfortable, but that doesn't mean we should shy away from it, does it? *(Beat. Laughs)* Yes, and it started with a tweet. Sounds like a bad song. How random is this. Well, maybe it's not. *(Beat)* Thanks, I didn't think anyone would read my reviews, but hey, I've got three hundred and sixty-three followers – and you, of course. *(Beat)* But I don't want to be a critic. I want to make TV that is meaningful, that surprises you with how it looks and acts on you, but I really want it to mean something when every time I turn on the—

ISOBEL enters. She has been cycling, sweaty. Helmet off.

ALEXANDRA   Sorry, got to go. *(Beat)* I know. It's just I feel we're just getting started and . . . *(Beat)*

OK. OK. Bye. *(Hangs up)* Hello. How many miles?

ISOBEL   Twenty.

ALEXANDRA   Slouch.

ISOBEL   I'm getting old.

ALEXANDRA   Keep pedalling.

ISOBEL   The great race you always lose in the end.

ALEXANDRA   Pedal pedal.

ISOBEL   That him from the other night?

ALEXANDRA   No.

ISOBEL   He was a bit short.

ALEXANDRA   For you?

ISOBEL   For you!

ALEXANDRA   Is this official questioning?

ISOBEL   OK. Is that short reply because it's an important guy or a very very *un*important guy?

ALEXANDRA   You're the cop.

ISOBEL   Yes, I am. How's the big project going?

ALEXANDRA   Makes it sound a little like a primary school insect-collecting trip.

ISOBEL   Sorry, didn't mean that. Bad mum.

ALEXANDRA   Yes, bad mum. If you want to know, I have
            started on something for my final project.
            It's edgy and I'm working with this person
            who I think could really open things up
            for me.

ISOBEL   That's fantastic.

ALEXANDRA   I know, I know. When you think someone's
            innocent or you get, you know, your cop
            hunch, you have to follow it, don't you?

ISOBEL   The only thing I have to follow is the law.

ALEXANDRA   I suppose that's the difference between art
            and police work. The truth lives behind the
            eyes of facts.

ISOBEL   That's good – you should use that in—

ALEXANDRA   Mum, you're being—

ISOBEL   I'm not condescending. I like it.

ALEXANDRA   Yeah? Should I write it down?

ISOBEL   Yes!

ALEXANDRA   What was it I said again?

ISOBEL   Now *my* mother if she heard you say that
            would say it must have been a lie.

ALEXANDRA   'The truth lives behind the eyes of facts.'
            Hmm.

ISOBEL   I have a fresh lasagne.

ALEXANDRA   Fresh from Tesco?

ISOBEL   Yes, I—

ALEXANDRA   Going out.

ISOBEL   Oh. Fine.

ALEXANDRA   Sorry.

ISOBEL   Is it him from last week, or someone else?

ALEXANDRA   It's Lilly and Mary, actually.

ISOBEL   Oh, OK.

ALEXANDRA   If that's OK with you.

ISOBEL   Fine, so probably alone, then?

ALEXANDRA   What?

ISOBEL   When you come back.

ALEXANDRA   Yes, probably.

ISOBEL   OK.

ALEXANDRA   There's loads of fat in lasagne.

ISOBEL   Do you think I'm getting fat?

ALEXANDRA   Yes.

ISOBEL   Oh.

ALEXANDRA   Sorry, was that too blunt?

ISOBEL   I can hardly complain.

ALEXANDRA   No, you can't.

ISOBEL   I'll save you some.

ALEXANDRA   Thanks.

ISOBEL   I got some green stuff to go with it.

ALEXANDRA   Well done.

ALEXANDRA takes up her iPad and notes and is about to head to her bedroom.

ISOBEL   Do I get an invite to the premiere?

ALEXANDRA   Of course you do.

ISOBEL   Anything wrong?

ALEXANDRA   No. I've made a breakthrough with this person and he's kind of the inspiration. My head is like jangling with ideas and images when I speak to him and I think there's a story there, it means something.

ISOBEL   Sounds great.

ALEXANDRA   This is my thing and I want you to support me in it.

ISOBEL   Of course I will.

ALEXANDRA   You were Scotland's first female chief constable and I want to make a mark too.

ISOBEL   Just being you.

ALEXANDRA Yes, but apart from the 'mother-love you're special whatever'. I can do things.

ISOBEL I know.

ALEXANDRA OK.

ISOBEL I'm sweaty.

ALEXANDRA Sorry about the lasagne.

ISOBEL Sorry I'm fat.

ALEXANDRA You're not.

ALEXANDRA exits. ISOBEL takes out a pile of cassettes, files, etc. It is CHALMERS' case files, photographs. ALEXANDRA comes back through. ISOBEL quickly packs them away.

ALEXANDRA Just heading out. Now who's being secretive?

ISOBEL Sorry.

ALEXANDRA What's the matter, Mum?

ISOBEL Nothing.

ALEXANDRA Mum?

ISOBEL I'm thinking of writing a book.

ALEXANDRA Great!

ISOBEL If I retire, maybe it's something that could bring a little extra money in.

ALEXANDRA   Great idea.

ISOBEL   Maybe.

ALEXANDRA   Not to be disrespectful, but why do you
            think a book would sell?

ISOBEL   First female chief constable in Scotland.

ALEXANDRA   OK, that's a newspaper article.

ISOBEL   Thanks.

ALEXANDRA   Just saying.

ISOBEL   Some interesting cases.

ALEXANDRA   *(Pointing to briefcase)* Like in there?

ISOBEL   Mm-hm.

ALEXANDRA   OK. Great.

ISOBEL   Are you OK with that?

ALEXANDRA   Am I in your book?

ISOBEL   Not written it yet, but no, it'll be purely
            police work.

ALEXANDRA   Well if I'm not in it, I've lost interest
            already. Good luck.

ISOBEL   Really?

ALEXANDRA   Got to go, Mum.

ISOBEL   Thanks.

ALEXANDRA   Right. Bye.

ISOBEL   Bye.

ALEXANDRA exits. ISOBEL takes a bunch of files including clippings, photographs, etc., and spreads them over the floor and table. They take over the room, with each place having its own particular zone: victims' photographs, press clippings, reports, etc.

ISOBEL   Lorraine. Rebecca. Lisa. Sarah. Dear God.
                There you are. Still there. Still gone.

She finally takes a cassette recorder out of her bag and puts it down, places one of the cassettes inside, hesitates, presses play. Nothing happens. She gets prickly skin and itches, rubs at her neck and arms. She picks up photographs of the four victims. She places them side by side.

ISOBEL   Sarah. Welcome home, Sarah. It's all done.
                It's only stories now. I won't disturb you,
                I hope.

CHALMERS   *(Voice from cassette. He has a cold and sniffs
                throughout)* Here we are again.

ISOBEL starts, swung back twenty years by the voice.

CHALMERS   *(Voice from cassette)* Have you found him
                yet?

ISOBEL   *(Voice from cassette)* Have we found who?

CHALMERS   *(Voice from cassette)* The man who killed
              those girls.

FRANK   *(Voice from cassette)* Oh yeah, we found him.

ISOBEL   *(Voice from cassette)* Interview begins eight
              thirty a.m. November the sixth, 1988.
              Present in the room are Alfred Chalmers,
              Chief Superintendent Fergus McLintock,
              Detective Inspector Frank Bowman and
              Detective Constable Isobel McArthur.

FERGUS   *(Voice from cassette)* When did you meet
              Lorraine Robertson?

CHALMERS   *(Voice from cassette)* I didn't. Have you got a
              tissue or something?

FERGUS   *(Voice from cassette)* But you were an orderly
              at the hospital where Miss Robertson was
              admitted for a termination.

CHALMERS   *(Voice from cassette)* There are many women
              come and go there, you should know that.

FERGUS   *(Voice from cassette)* And do you remember
              when you met Rebecca Telford?

CHALMERS   *(Voice from cassette)* No.

FERGUS   *(Voice from cassette)* Lisa Brown?

CHALMERS   *(Voice from cassette)* No.

FERGUS   *(Voice from cassette)* Sarah McElhenney?

CHALMERS   *(Voice from cassette)* Yes.

FERGUS   *(Voice from cassette)* When was that?

CHALMERS   *(Voice from cassette)* Early September, I think it was. You can check – the hospital will keep records.

FRANK   *(Voice from cassette)* Well fuck me, you're a real helpful c—

CHALMERS   *(Voice from cassette)* I really need something for my nose, could you . . .

ISOBEL   *(Voice from cassette)* Here.

CHALMERS   *(Voice from cassette)* Thank you.

FERGUS   *(Voice from cassette)* Did she stick in your mind?

CHALMERS   *(Voice from cassette)* Sorry.

FERGUS   *(Voice from cassette)* Well, you've forgotten about the others. What made Sarah stand out, do you think?

CHALMERS   *(Voice from cassette)* Sarah's the name of my daughter.

FERGUS   *(Voice from cassette)* These records at the hospital – do you have access to them?

CHALMERS   *(Voice from cassette)* No, only medical staff.

FERGUS   *(Voice from cassette)* Would it be possible for you to see them? Their addresses?

CHALMERS *(Voice from cassette)* I don't know, because I never tried.

ISOBEL   *(Voice from cassette)* What would you do if your Sarah turned up for an abortion at the hospital?

CHALMERS *(Voice from cassette)* Would never happen, not my Sarah.

ISOBEL   *(Voice from cassette)* How do you know?

CHALMERS *(Voice from cassette)* They came into the hospital like they were making a withdrawal from their bank.

ISOBEL   *(Voice from cassette)* What if they were raped?

CHALMERS *(Voice from cassette)* They weren't.

ISOBEL   *(Voice from cassette)* Weren't they?

CHALMERS *(Voice from cassette)* Well how would I know?

FRANK   *(Voice from cassette)* Good question, Alfred.

CHALMERS *(Voice from cassette)* If I say I know them, you do your evil maths and use it on me. I say I don't know them and you say I must. You've decided, because you want to win. I don't like what those girls did, no, I don't. And do you know why? Because

I think human life is sacred. Sacred. Now do your maths.

FRANK   *(Voice from cassette)* You're not maths, Chalmers. You're the mess that happens before maths.

CHALMERS   *(Voice from cassette)* I didn't kill those girls.

ISOBEL   *(Voice from cassette)* Even though they killed their babies?

CHALMERS   *(Voice from cassette)* That's right, provocative Isobel.

FRANK   *(Voice from cassette)* Good name, 'Provocative Isobel'.

CHALMERS   *(Voice from cassette suddenly loud, wild)*
You slimy fucking prick Frank flipping your stupid dumb-boy words like you mean something. You think you're funny but God help you if you ever lose the uniform because

ALEXANDRA enters unnoticed.

Frank you are a cunt because you have nothing on me and the reason you have nothing on me is because there is nothing *to* have on me because I didn't do it. *(Calmer now)* And you, Isobel, you want it to be me too much. And that is not right—

ISOBEL notices ALEXANDRA. She puts off the cassette.

ALEXANDRA   Sorry, forgot my purse, I—

ISOBEL   Sorry, it's an old case I'm—

ALEXANDRA   For your book?

ISOBEL   Yes, yes, for the book. Maybe, I don't know.

ALEXANDRA   *(Laughs)* You don't know?

ISOBEL   Still thinking.

ALEXANDRA   You can probably get something for that on eBay, you know.

ISOBEL   Sorry? Oh, OK, yes. Look, have a nice night.

ALEXANDRA picks up her purse. ISOBEL gathers up the files.

ISOBEL   Sorry about . . .

ALEXANDRA   Night.

ISOBEL   Night. Be safe.

ALEXANDRA   *(Laughs)* I'm always safe. My mother's chief of police!

ALEXANDRA exits. ISOBEL drops one of the photos on the floor. She looks at it. Uneasily she picks it up.

ISOBEL   Sarah. Sarah.

Blackout.

SCENE FOUR

*Midnight. Living room. There is the intermittent sound of
noisy sex coming from off. Phone rings. A tired ISOBEL
enters, drags herself to find the phone. Answers.*

ISOBEL   Hello. *(Pause)* Hello.

*She puts the phone down. She hears the sex. She pours
herself a whisky. She picks a file off the floor, places
another cassette in the player and reads as she listens.*

CHALMERS *(Voice from the cassette, sounding tired)*
             . . . whether the most important thing is
             what you do or maybe *why* you do what you
             do. You're keen, aren't you, Isobel. Keen to
             get on. The guys here see something in you,
             maybe something of the *man*.

FRANK   *(Voice from the cassette)* More of a man than
             you.

CHALMERS *(Voice from the cassette)* Or maybe they just
             want to have you.

FERGUS   *(Voice from the cassette)* Now, now, Alfred.

CHALMERS *(Voice from the cassette)* I don't want you to
             think I've anything against women . . .

FRANK   *(Voice from the cassette)* He's a stand-up!

CHALMERS   *(Voice from the cassette)* . . . but it must be
               hard with all these men and you must have
               to try that bit harder.

ISOBEL   *(Voice from the cassette)* Is that wrong?

CHALMERS   *(Voice from the cassette)* But you're so
               desperate to make your mark that you
               might just stare and stare till you see what
               you want to see. You might just push and
               push till you get what you think you want
               to get. And that's where it stops being
               clean.

ISOBEL   *(Voice from the cassette)* Can't the truth be
               messy?

CHALMERS   *(Voice from the cassette)* The truth *is* messy
               enough without your mess stuck all over
               it. Me connected with those women – a
               fact and a truth you are twisting to death
               to create the illusion that will gain you
               something, selfish girl. Meanwhile, the guys
               slip secret looks at you and get hard-ons—

*ISOBEL hears the sex get louder and turns up the volume
almost pettily.*

FERGUS   *(Voice from the cassette)* What do you know
               about the constellations?

CHALMERS   *(Voice from the cassette)* I'm Gemini. What
            are you?

FERGUS   *(Voice from the cassette)* 'It's in the stars' and
            'Look up'. What do you think that means?
            Why write that?

CHALMERS   *(Voice from the cassette)* No idea. Wrote that
            on them, did he?

ISOBEL   *(Voice from the cassette)* In blood on their
            stomachs. After we found your third victim,
            Lisa, we saw your pattern. The constellation
            of Cassiopeia: the Vain Queen. So we knew
            where the next victim would be found.

FRANK   *(Voice from the cassette)* Star 1, Lorraine
            Robertson, in an oil drum near the Junction
            of Ferry Road and Granton; Star 2, Rebecca
            Telford, in a tree under the Dean Bridge;
            Star 3, Lisa Brown, hanging on the railings
            around the Dugald Stewart Monument on
            Calton Hill; Star 4, not in pattern, hidden
            under the floorboards like a guilty secret.

CHALMERS   *(Voice from the cassette)* I don't know
            anything about stars!

FERGUS   *(Voice from the cassette)* What went wrong
            with Sarah, Alfred? Wasn't found where
            she should have been. Panic? And there are
            five stars in that constellation. That'll never
            happen now, will it?

CHALMERS   *(Voice from the cassette)* Piss off, Fergus.
            Your compass is broke and your science
            compromised. It found me and it lied.
            Because you invented this, not me. And
            you did this, not me.

*ALEXANDRA enters. She is drunk and with a dressing gown
wrapped around her.*

ALEXANDRA   Can you turn that down?

ISOBEL turns it off.

ISOBEL   Can you?

ALEXANDRA   Fuck off.

ISOBEL   I'll turn it down.

ALEXANDRA   What are you listening to him for?

ISOBEL   Him?

ALEXANDRA   It's him, isn't it? Chalmers.

ISOBEL   How did you know it was—

ALEXANDRA   Chalmers? Twenty-fifth anniversary of his
            arrest. You're writing a book. 'Biggest fish I
            ever caught.' You. Him.

ISOBEL   My book is of no interest to any publisher
            unless he's in it.

ALEXANDRA   He's your trophy serial killer.

ISOBEL   Maybe.

ALEXANDRA   Do you need to write a book?

ISOBEL   I want to write it.

ALEXANDRA   OK.

ISOBEL   Do you need to do your project?

ALEXANDRA   Good to talk.

ISOBEL   It's late to talk.

ALEXANDRA   Maybe it is.

ISOBEL   I meant late at night.

ALEXANDRA   Maybe it all started with him? *(Indicates
             tape recorder)*

ISOBEL   What did?

ALEXANDRA   I don't know. It.

ISOBEL   Honestly, Alex, you wear me out with your
             riddles.

A YOUNG MAN in boxers enters.

YOUNG MAN   You coming back, student Alex?

ALEXANDRA   Just wait in the bedroom.

YOUNG MAN   Cause my cock's ready for round two.
             (Sees ISOBEL) Oh, hello, Mum. Didn't know
             Mum was home. Oops.

ISOBEL   I'm not your mother. Just pretend I'm not
            here, why don't you.

ALEXANDRA   I didn't need to pretend. *(To YOUNG MAN)*
            Come on, Muhammad Ali. Let's see what
            you've got left.

*ALEXANDRA and YOUNG MAN exit. ISOBEL pours another
whisky. Throb of dance music from the next room. She
picks up files again, takes a laptop out and prepares to
write. She fast-forwards the cassette.*

ISOBEL   *(Voice from cassette)* . . . seventh interview
            with Alfred Chalmers. Date: November
            the nineteenth, 1988. Time: eight thirty-
            five p.m. Present: Detective Inspector
            Frank Bowman and Detective Constable
            Isobel McArthur. Where were you on the
            night of September the seventeenth? *(No
            response)* Records show you worked at the
            Royal Infirmary and finished your shift at
            seven p.m. that evening. Where did you go
            afterwards? *(No response)* Why did you put
            Sarah's body under her floorboards and
            not place it in public like the others? *(No
            response)*

ISOBEL   *(Looking at photographs)* Why put her in
            her own house? Why change the rules?
            Why was a strand of her clothing found on
            yours? How did that happen, Alfred?

FRANK   *(Voice from cassette)* It was clever what you did: you got the headlines just like you wanted, so now you can tell us the grand plan.

ISOBEL   *(Voice from cassette)* So they were all unemployed, they all had terminations. Am I being obvious, or is it just as simple as it seems?

ISOBEL   *(Shouting over the last bit of cassette dialogue)* Why did you change the rules? What happened? What—

CHALMERS   *(Shouting from cassette at live ISOBEL)* Why can't you think up some original questions after twenty-five bloody years? Do I need to listen to all this shit again?

ISOBEL   You never answered the questions.

CHALMERS   *(Voice from cassette)* You weren't clever enough to be rewarded with them.

ISOBEL   So what did those women do to be rewarded by you?

CHALMERS   *(Voice from cassette)* Stinking wasters. Do-nothingers, breed in bed and flush the consequences down the plug hole.

ISOBEL   You never put Sarah, your fourth, in the constellation. Why?

At this point CHALMERS is revealed stirring a large
saucepan full of tar.

CHALMERS   Look, I'm a bit busy right now: got to get
                this finished. No idea how my arm aches.
                Think stirring tar's easy? It's not. Got
                machines in builders'—

ISOBEL   Why not just kill them? Why hide her when
                you wanted the bodies to be found?

CHALMERS   Because it shone a light.

ISOBEL   On what? Why?

CHALMERS   On them. Creepy-crawlies. *(Giggles)*

ISOBEL   Did you watch them before you killed
                them?

CHALMERS   Of course. I am nothing if not thorough.
                If a job's worth doing . . .

ISOBEL   So you found out their addresses from the
                hospital records, you stalked them . . .

CHALMERS   Now, now, 'stalked' is a bit judgemental.

ISOBEL   And then when you felt safe, you murdered
                them.

CHALMERS   You think a woman can't stand up for
                herself, Constable Isobel?

ISOBEL   I'm a chief superintendent now.

CHALMERS   So you're better than that Constable Isobel back then?

ISOBEL   *(Voice from cassette)* Yes, Isobel, I think that's a bit much.

FRANK   *(Voice from cassette)* Bloody good copper you were too, Isobel, before you decided paperwork was your thing.

ISOBEL   Strategy, Frank. No strategy and we're all headless chickens.

FRANK   *(Voice from cassette)* You turned your back on the real work, dealing with people like him!

CHALMERS   He's got a point. I mean, you did catch me.

CHALMERS   *(Voice from cassette)* She caught the wrong person!

ISOBEL   *(Voice from cassette)* I caught the right person!

CHALMERS   Can I just get on with this, get it done and get some peace?

ISOBEL   OK, what's peace for you? What peace do you get when that girl stops breathing? What stops rattling in your head?

CHALMERS   Interference. White noise. All they are.

FRANK   *(Voice from cassette)* Can I hear someone fucking?

ISOBEL   Did something interrupt you taking her
                body out like the others?

CHALMERS   *(Voice from cassette)* Heard it all. She asked
                me that twenty-five years ago.

ISOBEL   *(Voice from cassette)* I did, actually.

FRANK   *(Voice from cassette)* I can definitely hear
                someone fucking. Isobel, is there someone
                having sex in the next room?

ISOBEL   Alexandra.

FRANK   *(Voice from cassette)* She's not even born yet.

ISOBEL   She is now. She's with Muhammad.

FRANK   *(Voice from cassette)* She's with a black guy?
                In Edinburgh? Fuck.

ISOBEL   No, not— shut up, Frank! What did the
                constellation mean? Cassiopeia?

CHALMERS   The Vain Queen.

ISOBEL   Yes.

CHALMERS   Can't help you.

ISOBEL   Why dump Sarah's body under the
                floorboards? It doesn't make sense.

CHALMERS   No, it doesn't, does it? This is disgusting.
                I shouldn't be doing this!

ISOBEL   So why are you?

CHALMERS   You're making me do it.

FRANK   *(Voice from cassette)* A black guy?

ISOBEL   But why?

CHALMERS   *(Finding a knife in his hand)* Have to do . . .
             what comes next.

ISOBEL   *(Voice from cassette)* Don't let him escape!

ISOBEL   Stop! Stop now!

CHALMERS   You can't stop me. It's already happened.

*The image of a person with a fox's head appears either
somewhere in the room or at the window of the house.
It is a bloody and disfigured mess with red eyes. Sex noises
a bit more focal.* CHALMERS *disappears/exits. Screams off.*
ISOBEL *sees* FOXHEAD. *Noise of sex from off suggesting
a move to climax at the end of dialogue.*

ISOBEL   What?

ISOBEL   *(Voice from cassette)* What is it? Have you let
             him go?

ISOBEL   Frank, there's something here with me, and
             it's not Chalmers.

ISOBEL	CHALMERS	FRANK
I am trying to make sense of this and I am facing up to the possibility . . .	Let me go! Let me go! You got the wrong man you fucking idiots. Let me go!	Shut up, you woman killer you scum.

FRANK   Those girls had nothing, and you took even that away from them.

CHALMERS   I didn't kill her. It wasn't me!

ISOBEL	CHALMERS	FRANK
No, I can't do this. We did it, we solved it, it's done – so why does it rattle about? Is it the book? Is it retiring?	It wasn't me. Invented me! Invented all this! All of it!	Come on, Isobel. Man up so those poor girls' mums and dads can sleep at night without – having their fucking daughters' tarred spangled faces screaming through their nightmares.

CHALMERS   It's all invented!

ISOBEL   Oh God. I don't want this back in my head
again.

*FOXHEAD makes noise as if alert to ISOBEL. Will it attack
or run? It holds a finger up, points at her, puts finger to
its lips (or thereabouts) and goes as ALEXANDRA and the
YOUNG MAN climax.*

SCENE FIVE

*FRANK, in ISOBEL's office. Sitting around waiting. JANICE
enters. She has some papers, puts them on ISOBEL's desk.
FRANK picks them up.*

FRANK   I'm waiting. For the chief.

JANICE   Is she expecting you?

FRANK   No.

JANICE   Do you want me to get Jenny? She's got her
          diary.

FRANK   No, Jenny can stand down for the moment.

JANICE   OK.

FRANK   You like your job?

JANICE   Yes, sir.

FRANK   Good, good. You like working for the chief?

JANICE   Yes, she's great.

FRANK   Yes, she is.

JANICE   Anything I can get you?

FRANK   Have you got any more of that stuff on
          Chalmers she's been asking for?

JANICE   No, she's got it all. There's nothing more.
           Are we thinking of reopening that case, sir?

FRANK   Over my dead body.

JANICE   So why—

ISOBEL enters.

ISOBEL   Janice.

JANICE   Ma'am.

ISOBEL   Aha! Frank, I don't have you in my diary.

FRANK   *(To JANICE)* Janice, can you speak to Jenny
           about this, because if the chief super doesn't
           have me in her diary and I'm running CID,
           then the consequences could be disastrous.

ISOBEL   You can go now, Janice.

JANICE   Thanks, ma'am.

FRANK   And tell Jenny, Janice, that I'll have a word
           before I go.

JANICE exits.

ISOBEL   You're not funny.

FRANK   Well I am a bit.

ISOBEL   She's good, and your games mess with her
           head.

FRANK   If she's that good, she can deal with it.

ISOBEL   And there is no CID any more.

FRANK   Words, Isobel, words.

ISOBEL   God, this is endless.

FRANK   You must love your job.

ISOBEL   I do love my job.

FRANK   I'd hate your job. Your job doesn't let you do
what you wanted to do when you signed up.

ISOBEL   Yes it does.

FRANK   No it doesn't.

ISOBEL   Do you need something? We'll be seeing each
other at our Thursday morning briefing.

FRANK   Our chat stayed with me. Maybe even worried
me a bit.

ISOBEL   You don't need to worry.

FRANK   Just strikes me as odd when you've got all
this stuff to deal with and you're asking your
protégé for files from a case that's closed and
twenty-five years old. Because I know what
I'm doing, Isobel. I'm dealing with the bad
stuff right now and also getting ready for the
next thing, so despite being – and I know I
may be called this, though never to my face –
a dinosaur, I am at least forward-thinking in
that respect.

ISOBEL   Who said I've been looking at files?

FRANK   A little bird told me.

ISOBEL   Don't stalk me.

FRANK   I'm not. But you're not alone with this, and you start dabbling then your fingers are going to touch me. Actually, that's not an all that unpleasant image.

ISOBEL   Nothing will interfere with my work.

FRANK   You sure?

ISOBEL   Don't fucking question me, Frank!

FRANK   God, you're sexy.

ISOBEL   You are in my office.

FRANK   *(Beat)* You sleeping OK?

ISOBEL   No, probably not.

FRANK   That's the start.

ISOBEL   If there's something to fix, is that wrong?

FRANK   *(Shouting)* There's nothing to fix.

ISOBEL   Maybe.

FRANK   Fuck 'maybe'. There's nothing to fix.

ISOBEL   Then why get so worked up?

FRANK   Because he messed us up then and he can do it again.

ISOBEL   He's inside.

FRANK   He's a virus – he's already out. You name him
          and he's out and he's in me and you and in
          Fergus.

ISOBEL   That's rubbish – you're inventing him as
          something—

FRANK   I'm calling it like it is.

ISOBEL   There's nothing he can do to us.

FRANK   Fergus had a stroke.

ISOBEL   When?

FRANK   Last night.

ISOBEL   Why? I mean, why didn't you tell me when you
          came in, instead of . . . instead of—

FRANK   Because I needed to talk a bit and I thought it
          might be you could—

ISOBEL   You know what he means to me.

FRANK   I don't know. What *does* he mean to you?

ISOBEL   How fucking dare you ask me that?

FRANK   Because I don't think you bringing all this up
          again is exactly the act of a friend, or even in
          fact a colleague.

ISOBEL   You've no right to say this to me.

FRANK Then who has? We were together then, in bed and at work.

ISOBEL That's in the past, Frank.

FRANK Can't you remember what it was like?

ISOBEL The sex?

FRANK What? No, not the sex. Though that too. That was then too. That time when we were investigating *him* and then when we got him. It got under our fingernails, it got up our nostrils; when I shat, I felt the worst of him go right through me. The universe is all dead-blood black and scattered with girls with no eyes. I wish we'd done him in and maybe that would have drawn a line.

ISOBEL A line under what?

FRANK Under *him*.

ISOBEL I don't think I ever have.

FRANK And now you're writing a book.

ISOBEL It's not about the book.

FRANK Alexandra's fees, is it?

ISOBEL It's about me.

FRANK You going to see him? *(Beat)* You've already seen him.

ISOBEL No.

FRANK   He wouldn't see you?

ISOBEL   He's agreed to meet.

FRANK   What does he want?

ISOBEL   It's me wants to see him. *I* want something.

FRANK   He wants something. If he's meeting you, he
          wants something.

ISOBEL   I'll give him a chance to talk.

FRANK   He had his chance. Why let him talk – people
          might end up listening. *Think!*

ISOBEL   I'm going on a hunch.

FRANK   That a cop hunch or a misplaced conscience
          hunch?

ISOBEL   I'm going on a hunch that something isn't –
          wasn't right.

FRANK   Fuck your hunch. Put it away.

ISOBEL   I can't – I don't have a choice.

FRANK   Of course you have a choice. You've got a brain,
          use it. You forgotten everything?

ISOBEL   No, I thought I could, but I can't, and
          everything – me thinking about retiring, the
          twenty-fifth anniversary of his arrest – it's like
          the planets are all aligning.

FRANK   Bullshit! Bullshit, Isobel. Just bullshit! No, no, no – the only alignments were the ones he made when he placed those girls' bodies all over this city and then razored what he did here. *(Taps his forehead)*

ISOBEL   And all that anger and pain, Frank, if it was so clear, how come we never got any evidence about the first three?

FRANK   Because he was clever.

ISOBEL   And we weren't?

FRANK   The fibre from her coat was on his jacket.

ISOBEL   For the fourth. For Sarah.

FRANK   For the fourth, Sarah, yeah, and he was the only fucking human being alive that knew all those four girls. Now tell me what your hunch said then and what it says now.

ISOBEL   Maybe he'll tell me the truth and I'll write it and we can all get clean.

FRANK   I don't need to, I'm OK with being dirty. It goes with the job. Man up, Isobel.

ISOBEL   Spoken like a—

FRANK   True friend.

ISOBEL   I can't let it go. I'm scared!

FRANK   No wonder. Jesus Christ, no wonder. Do you
          care for your book or your conscience more
          than me, more than Black Fergus?

ISOBEL   Yes.

DREW enters. Beat.

DREW   Just a signature. Jenny says you have
          Strathclyde at the desk, he's on his way up.

ISOBEL   Not Strathclyde now; the Chief Constable of
          Scot—

DREW   Sorry, ma'am.

ISOBEL   So was I.

DREW exits.

FRANK   He can't speak much, but he's stable. At the
          Royal Infirmary. Ward 7 on the east wing if you
          want to visit him.

ISOBEL   Of course I want to visit him.

FRANK   I'm sure he'll be glad to see you, even though
          last time you . . . *You're* scared? You scare the
          fuck out of me, Isobel.

*FRANK exits. ISOBEL sits. Picks up a cup and smashes it.
JANICE re-enters.*

ISOBEL   Just a mug, Janice.

JANICE   Oh, right.

ISOBEL   It deserved it.

JANICE   *(Beat then)* I thought we just arrested people.
Didn't think we carried out sentences.

ISOBEL   That mug was never going to be any good,
Constable Harker, but technically of course you
are right.

JANICE   I understand.

ISOBEL   Do you? Do I?

JANICE   Shall I get rid of the evidence?

ISOBEL   That would be lovely.

JANICE picks up the pieces.

ISOBEL   Do you want to be me, Janice?

JANICE   I want to be me, ma'am.

ISOBEL   That's a good answer. I have a daughter couple
of years younger than you.

JANICE   Don't be surprised if she doesn't want to be you
either.

ISOBEL   No. Why does nobody want to be me? What's
wrong with me?

JANICE   You're great, ma'am. Shall I dispose of the . . .
          er, the . . .

ISOBEL   Quietly, where no one can find it.

JANICE   As good as done.

ISOBEL   Thank you. I wonder . . .

JANICE   Yes?

ISOBEL   What am I going to drink my coffee out of now?

JANICE exits. ISOBEL presses a button on her phone.

ISOBEL   Jenny?

JENNY   *(Voice)* Ma'am?

ISOBEL   Cancel all my meetings Friday afternoon.

JENNY   *(Voice)* But you've got—

ISOBEL   Just do it, please.

JENNY   Yes, ma'am.

Blackout.

SCENE SIX

We should be able to see ALEXANDRA and CHALMERS.
She in ISOBEL's living room. He in the meeting room.
She has her mobile phone, he uses a landline.

CHALMERS   You're ten minutes late.

ALEXANDRA   Sorry, I—

CHALMERS   It's not easy to do this, so you need to keep time.

ALEXANDRA   I'm sorry.

CHALMERS   If it's not fixed and clear, it doesn't work. Don't you understand where I am? It has to happen exactly like I say or it doesn't work – those are the rules!

ALEXANDRA   OK.

CHALMERS   *(Beat)* I'm sorry I shouted at you. Being in here can make you vulnerable to the worst parts of you.

ALEXANDRA   It's OK, it's my fault. Maybe we shouldn't even be doing this.

CHALMERS   But Alexandra, it's you who asked for *my* help.

ALEXANDRA   I know.

CHALMERS   And I have engaged honestly with you.

ALEXANDRA   I appreciate that.

CHALMERS   Thank you for not abandoning me when
             I told you who I really was.

ALEXANDRA   I know I'm really on the edge doing this. I
             mean, my mum ... But this *is* where I want
             to be, talking about real things, revealing
             things, and I don't know if you can do that
             without risking breaking things.

CHALMERS   How much I hear your mother rise up in
             you at times.

ALEXANDRA   Do you hate me?

CHALMERS   No.

ALEXANDRA   You think that's what Mum did to you?

CHALMERS   Not absolutely. She didn't risk. Not like you.

ALEXANDRA   Just broke.

CHALMERS   We all break things. That drive you have,
             passion, youth and genes – you have the
             chance to define yourself.

ALEXANDRA   Crash – bang!

CHALMERS   Possibly. I completely understand why your
             mother did what she did. She thought she
             was right.

ALEXANDRA   But you think . . . I mean, you know she
            was wrong. You must hate her.

CHALMERS   I did hate her, blackly. But now I would like
            her to understand what she did.

ALEXANDRA   If we do this, she will.

CHALMERS   She might. And my family, Alexandra.

ALEXANDRA   I think I'm close to a structure for the
            documentary. I need your voice, though.

CHALMERS   That's tricky.

ALEXANDRA   I mean, there are these tapes with you
            speaking on that Mum's playing, but
            I don't think I can use them. Probably
            confidential.

CHALMERS   Probably.

JUDITH   *(Entering – to CHALMERS)* One minute.

ALEXANDRA   In the piece, I hear your voice and it's
            important.

CHALMERS   She's listening to the interview tapes?

ALEXANDRA   Has she been to see you?

CHALMERS   She's asked to talk to me. Has she got the
            case files with her?

ALEXANDRA   I don't know! It's just fucking typical.
            Amazingly, we meet, or make contact

through you following me on Twitter, I get
this great idea and there she is . . .

CHALMERS   Do you know what your mum is up to?

ALEXANDRA   Are you going to meet her? I know this can
work.

CHALMERS   Nobody ever knows if something will work.

JUDITH   Time, Alfred.

CHALMERS   Time's up: got to go. Goodbye.

ALEXANDRA   Bye . . . Bye.

She puts the phone down. Blackout.

SCENE SEVEN

FRANK revealed in ISOBEL's office. DREW enters.

FRANK   Where is she?

DREW   She's not here.

FRANK   Is that right?

DREW   Sorry.

FRANK   The future is in good hands with you now, isn't it? Do you know where she is?

DREW   She's taken the afternoon off.

FRANK   Right. Know why?

DREW   Getting a spray tan?

JANICE   *(Off)* Drew. We're moving. You need to be there now!

DREW hesitates.

FRANK   Well go then. Get the bad guys.

DREW   Sir.

He exits. FRANK paces, examines the desk. Nothing. Blackout.

SCENE EIGHT

A private room with a table, two chairs and security camera. JUDITH shows ISOBEL in. She is in civilian clothes.

JUDITH   I'll get him now. Take a seat.

ISOBEL   Thanks.

JUDITH goes. ISOBEL gets up and walks around the room. Her phone rings.

ISOBEL   *(Into phone)* Hello? *(Beat)* No, no, it's fine.
(Beat) I know it's a peaceful protest, just keep them on George Street, it—

She hears a noise off.

ISOBEL   Can't talk, I'll call later.

She hangs up. ALFRED CHALMERS enters with JUDITH. He is in his sixties, grey, but the face has great definition. There is nothing amorphous about it. He sits down. No one speaks for a bit.

ISOBEL   Hello, Alfred. *(Beat)* You're looking well. *(Beat)* I appreciate you seeing me. And I'm sure you're wondering . . . why is she here? Why *am* I here? I suppose any kind of anniversary makes you think back to what was at the beginning, the thing that started it. And then you think of yourself and whether you've changed, not just older, but have the values changed, can you see things now that you couldn't then, appreciate things now that you couldn't then. And here we are again. Me. You.

CHALMERS   Still positively self-obsessed, I see: in that respect you have not changed.

ISOBEL   Aren't we all self-obsessed?

CHALMERS   I wasn't until I was put here, and then I found being self-obsessed preferable – *(To JUDITH)* no offence – to any kind of interest in those who surrounded me.

ISOBEL   I suppose so, it—

CHALMERS   You see, that's the worst of it – it's not the walls or the nurses; it's the fact that they hole you up with you. And twenty-five years is such a long time.

ISOBEL   It is.

CHALMERS   Oh you don't know the half of it.

ISOBEL   We've all had our journeys.

CHALMERS   Except I was denied mine.

ISOBEL   *(Beat)* Are you well?

CHALMERS   Do you mean physically?

ISOBEL   Yes.

CHALMERS   Yes. Because the court thought I must be
            mad, remember.

ISOBEL   I remember. Would you be prepared to
            talk to me?

CHALMERS   About?

ISOBEL   The whole thing?

CHALMERS   With you?

ISOBEL   With me.

CHALMERS   What's this?

ISOBEL   What do you mean?

CHALMERS   You got a wire?

ISOBEL   It's not American TV.

CHALMERS   Are you reopening my case?

ISOBEL   No. Not yet.

CHALMERS   Not yet?

ISOBEL   It depends.

CHALMERS   On what?

ISOBEL   Whether you give me a reason to.

CHALMERS   Is there new evidence?

ISOBEL   No.

CHALMERS   Well there never was any old evidence,
was there, Chief Constable – sorry,
Superintendent, Isobel McArthur. Didn't
get that job, did you? *(Beat)* I don't have
many visitors.

ISOBEL   No?

CHALMERS   Yes, funny, that.

ISOBEL   That must be difficult.

CHALMERS   Don't identify with me. You can't. I haven't
seen my wife or daughter in twenty-five
years. Not even a letter or a postcard.
I suppose I don't blame them, either of
them. I don't really hold them responsible.
How would you feel if your daughter
disappeared?

ISOBEL   How do you know I've got a daughter?

CHALMERS   Do you?

ISOBEL   *(Beat)* Yes.

CHALMERS   Right.

ISOBEL	You're here because I am interested in the truth. Are you interested in the truth?
CHALMERS	Depends on whose it is.
ISOBEL	Yours? I'm thinking of retiring.
CHALMERS	Thank God. Innocent people can once again sleep in peace at night.
ISOBEL	I thought I might write a book.
CHALMER	Why would that interest anybody?
ISOBEL	Maybe it won't.
CHALMERS	Except . . .
ISOBEL	Yes?
CHALMERS	Except if it had me in it.
ISOBEL	You are part of the journey.
CHALMERS	No, Isobel, I *am* your journey.
ISOBEL	You're part of it.
CHALMERS	What's on the tip of your tongue, Isobel? Something's desperate to get out but you won't let it.
ISOBEL	I am open to whatever you—
CHALMERS	Yes, yes, well that's a surprise, you open to me telling you things to sell your book.
ISOBEL	Does it matter, if it's about truth?

CHALMERS Whose truth? You can't invent the truth.

ISOBEL I don't want to invent the truth.

CHALMERS But you sound like you've lost yours.

ISOBEL No, I haven't.

CHALMERS Now you want mine. And what for? What's in it for me?

ISOBEL Tell the world.

CHALMERS Tell the world what?

ISOBEL Your story.

CHALMERS Seeing you again. You're plain. Forgive me – hopefully you're past any vanity now. I can imagine you age of seven, waiting for Bobby Cefferty to choose you for the Gay Gordons. But he didn't. Went elsewhere. That other girl, remember her?

ISOBEL Sadly, yes.

CHALMERS Not sadly. That was the moment you realised that to be seen poor Isobel might need a lift to shine out.

ISOBEL Is that how you started?

CHALMERS Started? Is that the need? To be seen? To be seen to be right?

ISOBEL I'm interested in justice. I don't care if I'm right.

CHALMERS   I have to say, bit insensitive not caring
            about being right, when I was sent down for
            you believing you were right.

ISOBEL   It wasn't just me, and there was evidence.

CHALMERS   My God, wobbly-kneed eighties forensics
            stumbling across the great divide of theory
            and hard-line evidence.

ISOBEL   You had her on you.

CHALMERS   Fibres. A few fibres. Not under fingernails
            but on my jacket. God, it sounded so
            scientific and sophisticated at the trial.

ISOBEL   You knew her.

CHALMERS   She was a patient where I worked as an
            orderly.

ISOBEL   It all added up.

CHALMERS   It isn't maths. It's not arithmetic in the
            classroom.

ISOBEL   Really?

CHALMERS   Is this it?

ISOBEL   Is this what?

CHALMERS   Just realised we might have started.

ISOBEL   Maybe we have.

CHALMERS   Don't fuck about with me. I'm not stupid.

ISOBEL   OK.

CHALMERS   Glib little answers. Don't you degrade me.

ISOBEL   I won't.

CHALMERS   Don't you degrade me any more than you
             already have done.

ISOBEL   I didn't degrade you.

CHALMERS   There's nothing you got I want.

ISOBEL   We talk, something is said, maybe it's good
             for you.

CHALMERS   Glib.

ISOBEL   I'm not promising anything, I'm not
             working for you here, but I *am* going to tell
             a story, and you're in it.

CHALMERS   It's my anniversary. But then you know
             that.

ISOBEL   And so someone might pay for this book.
             But maybe only now. Think.

CHALMERS   Can't have done much in the last twenty-
             five, eh? You want me to celebrate your old
             victory over me?

ISOBEL   It's not like that.

CHALMERS   I didn't do it.

(Beat)

ISOBEL   If we talk, then—

CHALMERS   Any of them.

ISOBEL   You say.

CHALMERS   I say.

ISOBEL   Then talk. Does a fox's head mean anything
            to you?

CHALMERS   A what?

ISOBEL   Someone in a . . . in a mask, fox, I think.

CHALMERS   No. Should it?

ISOBEL   I just get this picture of . . . it's stupid.

CHALMERS   I've thought about you a lot, and they are
            not nice thoughts.

ISOBEL   OK.

CHALMERS   Just being honest.

ISOBEL   I can take that.

CHALMER   Stop with the glib shit, or I walk.

ISOBEL   I'm sorry. I get it. I think about you too, and
            they are not nice thoughts.

CHALMERS   This meeting is about to end. You don't
            interest me, at least not face to face
            anyways.

ISOBEL   What does that mean?

CHALMERS   Ding dong, finished. *(To JUDITH)* Take me to my room, please.

ISOBEL   It's an opportunity.

CHALMERS   You had an opportunity and it was twenty-five years ago. But you took another road.

ISOBEL   I took the road I believed in.

CHALMERS   You're here to gloat and make money out of my lost years. All that life I could have had that you and your lot flattened!

He starts to leave.

ISOBEL   Isn't there anything you want said?

CHALMERS   Tell me if you have a doubt.

ISOBEL   What?

CHALMERS   Tell me if you have a doubt. About me.

ISOBEL   In what way?

CHALMERS   Going.

ISOBEL   There's lots of doubts around the case, we—

CHALMERS   Do you have a doubt or not?

ISOBEL   That you killed them?

CHALMERS   Yes, yes, that's right.

ISOBEL   I arrested you.

CHALMERS   Any doubt?

ISOBEL   I gave evidence at the trial. They were
             facts, it's not about—

CHALMERS   Is it there? Is there any doubt? Is there?
             Going, going, g—

ISOBEL   Yes.

CHALMERS   Thank you, Isobel. *(To JUDITH)* My room
             now, please. My room now.

CHALMERS exits, leaving ISOBEL alone.

SCENE NINE

ISOBEL arrives back at the same time as ALEXANDRA in a dressing gown or towel is taking the bag of files into the living room. It's a kind of collision that neither of them wants or was expecting.

ISOBEL   I thought you'd be at uni.

ALEXANDRA   I thought you'd be at work. Were you?

ISOBEL   Yes.

ALEXANDRA   Home early?

ISOBEL   Yes. That OK?

ALEXANDRA   Why shouldn't it be?

ISOBEL   Well that's good then, isn't it? How's the project going?

ALEXANDRA   Wow.

ISOBEL   What?

ALEXANDRA   Never heard a question so uninterested in getting an answer.

ISOBEL   I do want to know.

ALEXANDRA   Let's not do this.

ISOBEL   What's that, love?

ALEXANDRA   Are you here? When you're here, are you
            here? The talk that isn't a talk. I'm fluent
            in talking to you in your absence.

ISOBEL   What does that mean?

ALEXANDRA   It means I am so mixed up about when you
            were actually here when I was young but
            not here. And then sometimes not here
            at all.

ISOBEL   What are you talking about: is this
            postmodernist talk?

ALEXANDRA   I don't know what it is, Mum.

ISOBEL   I'm trying to do something that is
            important to me.

ALEXANDRA   So am I.

ISOBEL   I know. I'd love to see what you've got so far.

ALEXANDRA   Not yet. God, even now, when you've
            achieved everything, you're still grabbing
            for it.

ISOBEL   Grabbing for what?

ALEXANDRA   The centre.

ISOBEL   It's not about that.

ALEXANDRA   Well you tell me what it is you're trying to
            solve, Chief Superintendent Isobel. What's
            it about?

ISOBEL   It's about trying to understand what I've
            been doing for thirty years.

ALEXANDRA   That sounds like a big fat me.

ISOBEL   It's a book. Money. Maybe a wee bit of
            salvation.

ALEXANDRA   Do you need that? Salvation?

ISOBEL   Maybe that's why I'm writing the book.
            How could you say that!

ALEXANDRA   Say what, Mum?

ISOBEL   About me being the centre of things.

ALEXANDRA   I only meant you being the centre of you.
            You see, you had to have actually been
            there to be at the centre of my world.

ISOBEL   Oh I was there, Alexandra.

ALEXANDRA   I can't fix you in my past sometimes. I
            sometimes see us sitting at the dinner table
            but then you're not there. Where were you?
            Was it actually me alone at the dinner
            table?

ISOBEL   I was there. It's the stress—

ALEXANDRA   But then I have a keen memory of you with
             a three-tiered jelly, all circus colours.

ISOBEL   You see – you might even have had fun in
             your childhood.

*The sound of music suddenly kicks up in the room off. We
can hear a man whooping, mock-rapping along. ISOBEL
and ALEXANDRA look at each other for a while.*

ISOBEL   So that's why you're not at uni.

ALEXANDRA   You're going to write about *him*. He's your
             star, isn't he?

ISOBEL   He's a part of it.

ALEXANDRA   Big part?

ISOBEL   At the moment, he's a significant part, yes.

ALEXANDRA   A monster?

ISOBEL   Could be.

ALEXANDRA   Don't you know? Well if he's not, then who's
             the monster?

*A knocking at the door. ALEXANDRA mouths along
to the music off and slowly withdraws to the bedroom.
ISOBEL looks about her, seeing the files. She grabs
some and puts them in a pile somewhere, leaving
the others to lie. She answers the door. It is Frank.
He is drunk and staggers inside.*

FRANK   I know it's early, but I had the afternoon off, and there's the Alhambra in Leith where irresponsible men go: so I went and it was uncomfortable – for them, owing to me having done them over a range of misdemeanours – but I did get served, and kept getting served and then it went a bit blurry.

ISOBEL   Do come in, Frank.

FRANK   *(Puzzled)* I *am* in. Been a while. Suddenly remembered. Fuck. This place. You live here. You fucking—

ISOBEL   Not into this, Frank.

FRANK   I know, but—

ISOBEL   And you said you'd never bring it up, so if you are so drunk that you can't keep your word, then get out.

FRANK   Sorry. I'm done now. Two people. You and me. Alone.

ISOBEL   I'm not alone.

FRANK   Yes, I know you've got Alex, but you know. How is Alex, by the way?

ISOBEL   She lacks any drive other than a sex drive.

FRANK   So normal, then?

ISOBEL   No, Frank, I don't think so.

FRANK   You can't remember? See, I did try. I got
         married. But I don't know that I should have.
         How many years was I miserable? How long
         was she miserable, poor cow? Poor cow who
         takes my money with a little flat on North
         Berwick High Street and manages to keep
         busy by book clubs and the Shipwrecked
         Fishermen and Mariners' Royal Benevolent
         Society. Do fishermen still get shipwrecked?

ISOBEL   Yes.

FRANK   And even though it is an absolutely brilliant
         fact that she is gone, her leaving has not led to
         . . . to the next thing.

ISOBEL   Go home, Frank.

FRANK   What's at home?

ISOBEL   Sky Sports.

FRANK   Oh, you're good.

ISOBEL   I know.

FRANK   Men go into their caves. Shamed by our
         thinning hair, springless knees and whatnot.
         My penis still works, though – it's still tip-top.

ISOBEL   That's just wonderful for you, Frank.

FRANK   Thanks, Isobel. I'll pass it on.

ISOBEL   By all means.

FRANK   Unless you'd like to say it personally.

ISOBEL   No, I trust you with the message.

FRANK   If you're sure.

ISOBEL   I'm sure.

FRANK   Right.

ISOBEL   My oh my. That felt a little close to the edge,
         Frank. Where did that come from?

FRANK   *(Examining the windows)* Should put locks on
         this.

ISOBEL   This is Merchiston, Frank.

FRANK   We could do it here.

ISOBEL   What?

FRANK   On the couch. Now.

ISOBEL   No.

*FRANK makes a move on her. It's not rough but drunkenly
direct.*

FRANK   Come on.

ISOBEL   No!

FRANK tries again.

FRANK   Come on. It's a good thing. It's a good thing.

ISOBEL   Get off! Stop it. Where did that come from? We
         haven't for, for—

FRANK   Nearly twenty-five years. You know, maybe it
         just brings it all back, Isobel. Maybe I thought,
         well, if the bad shit like him is on its way back
         up, then maybe some of the good things from
         then could be too. Because it was good, Isobel.

ISOBEL   Not so good that it lasted.

FRANK   So you can revisit *that*. *(Indicates files or
         cassettes)* But you can't *this*.

ISOBEL   That's right. There is nothing unresolved about
         us, Frank.

FRANK   Well maybe it's not about something being
         unresolved; maybe it's how I feel now, on this
         day, at this time.

ISOBEL   So you come round here for what? For a shag
         and a—

FRANK   Because I needed comfort and I thought you
         might be the only one to give it to me.

ISOBEL   You'd have screwed me and what?

FRANK   Tea and toast?

ISOBEL   Can't believe you're saying this. Go home and
         have a wank, Frank, you'll feel better.

FRANK   Can't you remember what it was like?

ISOBEL   Frank, it's . . . We are friends.

FRANK   Friends?

ISOBEL   *(Firm)* Friends, yes.

FRANK   Right. *(Beat)* I called at the office today.

ISOBEL   I wasn't there.

FRANK   You weren't there.

ISOBEL   Ah-ha.

FRANK   OK.

ISOBEL   OK.

FRANK   I like your young copper, what's her name?

ISOBEL   Janice.

FRANK   Janice, that's it.

ISOBEL   Bit young for—

FRANK   I'm not a hound dog, Isobel.

ISOBEL   That reference is your father's generation.

FRANK   He's still the King.

ISOBEL   His fat death happened nearly forty years ago.

FRANK   Don't take it out on Elvis, Isobel.

ISOBEL   I'm sorry, Frank.

The sound of sex in the next room.

FRANK   That's a bit . . .

ISOBEL   Yes.

FRANK   How do you . . . ?

ISOBEL   Well, you just do.

FRANK   It's your house.

ISOBEL   It's our house. It's pretty relentless. Frank, I saw Chalmers. I know you'd want to know and I think it's reasonable that I tell you. I met him.

FRANK   Right.

ISOBEL   Right?

FRANK   Well, what can I say?

ISOBEL   What you think.

FRANK   I've told you that. You still did it.

ISOBEL   I think he wants to tell the truth.

FRANK   Does he?

ISOBEL   I think so.

FRANK   And you'd trust Chalmers with something so precious as the truth?

ISOBEL   I need the truth.

FRANK   You had . . . you *have* the truth.

ISOBEL   I don't know.

FRANK   You do know.

ISOBEL   What wrong can come of this, Frank? I mean,
           it's talk.

FRANK   What wrong can come of it? Hasn't it already
           started?

ISOBEL   What . . . ?

FRANK   I got to call you on this, Isobel, and beg, and
           not for entirely altruistic reasons, that you
           stop this.

ISOBEL   I hear you. No.

FRANK   Right.

ISOBEL   You could help me.

FRANK   You're joking.

ISOBEL   I don't understand why—

FRANK   Because he's a nightmare, Isobel. The *idea*
           of him stinks up the place and people start
           choking. He sends a sliver of metal screaming
           through your nervous system. He's like some
           kind of fucked-up high. I like golf and I like
           getting the people who are about to do crime
           before they get a chance. And if I can't, then
           I'll get them after. That's my sworn duty. And
           that's my life. It might be small and not very
           wide, but it gets me up in the morning, maybe
           not always with a smile on my face, but I

know why my life is moving forward and as a consequence I can pay my maintenance and my Sky Sports package.

ALEXANDRA has appeared at the doorway.

ALEXANDRA   Thought I heard voices. Hello, Uncle Frank.

FRANK   Hello . . . God, you've grown up.

ALEXANDRA   You saw me six months ago. Just thought I'd check by in case Mum had brought back any strange men.

FRANK   Only me . . .

ALEXANDRA   Have you offered Uncle Frank a drink yet, Mum?

ISOBEL   I think Frank's had enough.

FRANK   Depends.

ALEXANDRA   Look at all the homework Mum has, Uncle Frank, she's got even more than me.

ISOBEL   What's got into you?

ALEXANDRA   Well . . .

ISOBEL   I've got to get some air.

ALEXANDRA   There's some outside.

ISOBEL   Thanks. ·

ALEXANDRA   Not much inside.

ISOBEL starts to exit.

ALEXANDRA   We'll get a pizza later, or have you—

ISOBEL   Sorry.

ALEXANDRA   No, it's OK.

ISOBEL   No, it's not, I should—

ALEXANDRA   Ah, should.

ISOBEL   Yes.

ALEXANDRA   *(Playful)* Old should've.

ISOBEL   Going.

ALEXANDRA   OK.

FRANK   Go, it's fine. Listen, don't forget Fergus. He's still in there.

ISOBEL   Shit.

FRANK   Yeah.

ALEXANDRA   Happy walking.

ISOBEL   Love you.

ISOBEL exits.

ALEXANDRA   You too. Is she allowed to bring all that home with her? Is this strictly legal, Frank?

FRANK   Strictly?

ALEXANDRA   Yes, strictly, by letter of law.

FRANK   No.

ALEXANDRA   Then why not arrest her?

FRANK   Because this is all . . . It's all done, it's nothing.

ALEXANDRA   Then why has Chief Superintendent McArthur filled her house with all this nothing?

FRANK   It'll pass.

ALEXANDRA   You sure?

FRANK   She's just trying to sort things out.

ALEXANDRA   Well, good to know she's keeping busy.

FRANK   You show your mum a little respect now, Alex.

ALEXANDRA   What was that?

FRANK   She deserves your respect. Your mum is . . . is substantial.

ALEXANDRA   She's not that fat.

FRANK   You know, Alex, don't be so light with things – you can lose them that way.

ALEXANDRA   Ooooh. Deep. Deep deep. Reminds me – better go. Lovely seeing you, Uncle Frank.

FRANK   Don't try and be so clever, Alexandra.
Stay innocent as long as you can.

ALEXANDRA   She's visiting Alfred Chalmers, isn't she?

FRANK   Yes.

ALEXANDRA   Do you think it's a good thing?

FRANK   No, I don't.

ALEXANDRA   Not good to check the past for truth and lies?

FRANK   That's a dark road. Your mum loves you. She's only ever done what she thinks was best for you. That's all you need to know.

ALEXANDRA   I don't know, Uncle Frank, I don't know how much I really believe that. I think she did what was best for her. I think that's what she always does. That's what I think even if I don't want to think it.

FRANK   That's a shame.

YOUNG MAN   *(Off)* Come on, Alexandra!

FRANK   It'll be OK. Nothing bad is going to happen.

ALEXANDRA   You make it sound like something might.

FRANK   No.

YOUNG MAN   *(Off)* Alexandra!

ALEXANDRA   Coming! Uncle Frank?

FRANK Yes?

ALEXANDRA I'd like you to fuck off now.

FRANK Sure, Alex.

FRANK goes to leave.

YOUNG MAN *(Off)* Come on!

FRANK If you need anything, you know, just—

ALEXANDRA I know. Thanks.

FRANK exits. ALEXANDRA picks up a file, looks at it.

YOUNG MAN *(Off)* Alexandra. Alexandra, I'm lonely. I'm soooo lonely.

ALEXANDRA Coming.

ALEXANDRA exits.

Act Two

SCENE ONE

ALEXANDRA alone. House. Quiet. CHALMERS on the phone.

CHALMERS   On time.

ALEXANDRA   Hello.

CHALMERS   *(Pause)* Are you still there?

ALEXANDRA   Yes.

CHALMERS   Don't you want to talk?

ALEXANDRA   I don't know.

CHALMERS   Has something upset you?

ALEXANDRA   I want to commit.

CHALMERS   Good.

ALEXANDRA   I mean to this. I'll do everything to make it happen.

CHALMERS   That's good.

ALEXANDRA   That is, if you still want to. *(Beat)* Do you?

CHALMERS   I have to think of my situation, Alexandra.

ALEXANDRA   I knew it, she's going to fuck this up for me.
            She's completely self-obsessed.

CHALMERS   If she is rethinking or even looking at
            my case then that could be significant in
            making things happen for me.

ALEXANDRA   I thought that's what *we* were doing.

CHALMERS   Of course, but Alexandra, your mother is
            the chief superintendent of Edinburgh
            police, and the person who arrested me.

ALEXANDRA   And I'm a flaky student making a
            documentary. If we get this right, it could
            open everything right up. I won't let you
            down. You're not going to dump me, are you?

CHALMERS   No.

ALEXANDRA   She wins again. OK, let's drop it.

CHALMERS   Wait! How would it be if I send you some
            spoken words?

ALEXANDRA   How?

CHALMERS   The post.

ALEXANDRA   Can you do that?

CHALMERS   I'm sure I can find a way.

ALEXANDRA   OK.

CHALMERS   I'll put some thoughts down about . . . then.
Would that help move things on?

ALEXANDRA   Yes. Yes, it would.

CHALMERS   OK.

ALEXANDRA   Do you want my address?

CHALMERS   Would be useful.

Pause as **ALEXANDRA** *hesitates.*

CHALMERS   Or we could forget it.

ALEXANDRA   No, no I—

CHALMERS   I'm not interested in not being trusted. You
say you want me to trust you, but you're
not sure about giving me your address?

ALEXANDRA   It's 121 Polwarth Gardens EH11 1LQ. *(Beat.
A little panicked)* Hello, are you still there,
Alfred?

CHALMERS   Is this a joke?

ALEXANDRA   No. What's wrong?

CHALMERS   Are you playing with me?

ALEXANDRA   No, what's wrong?

CHALMERS   That's interesting. Now that's a subject for
a book, Alexandra.

ALEXANDRA   What do you mean?

CHALMERS   I liked your last blog on the film festival.

ALEXANDRA   It's just words. Our piece will use visuals.
            What did you mean about my address?

CHALMERS   Nothing. Any pieces of paper hanging about
            with her thoughts written on them? You
            could look now.

ALEXANDRA   But—

CHALMERS   It's important to me.

ALEXANDRA   *(Moves to the files and picks them up)* Just the
            case files. She circled a couple of things;
            well, it looks fresh.

CHALMERS   Yes?

ALEXANDRA   'Sample fibre from victim's clothing found
            on suspect.' She's written 'Find' next to it.
            She's got all … all the four victims, with
            a column for each and lots of stuff about
            them. There's a dark line between Sarah
            McElhenney and the other ones.

CHALMERS   That's very useful, Alexandra, thank you.
            Let's keep talking.

ALEXANDRA   Oh, do you have to go? I was just going to
            give you my first storyboard ideas – though
            what you send me might change that, so—

CHALMERS   Let's talk when you get what I send you.

ALEXANDRA What? Oh, right. Exciting.

CHALMERS Yes, it's exciting. It's on the move.

ALEXANDRA What is? Right. Right.

CHALMERS hangs up. Blackout.

SCENE TWO

ISOBEL revealed, sitting at her desk. It's hard to tell whether she is sleeping or thinking. JANICE enters, stands unsure as to whether to enter properly. Finally . . .

JANICE   Ma'am? Ma'am?

ISOBEL   Yes?

JANICE   Are you all right?

ISOBEL   What is it, Janice?

JANICE   Inspector Ryan wants to know if he can talk about the Prince Harry visit.

ISOBEL   Does he? Yes, but not with me.

JANICE   *(Beat)* Right, I'll tell him then.

ISOBEL   A minute, Janice. Have you been on to Records about the forensics sample from the Chalmers case?

JANICE   They're looking, I think.

ISOBEL   'I think' offers nothing to me. How hard is it to find? Check again.

JANICE   Will do, ma'am. Do you want a coffee?

ISOBEL   I would kill for a coffee.

JANICE   That might put me in a difficult position.

ISOBEL laughs, then JANICE. FRANK knocks and enters.

FRANK   Morning.

ISOBEL   Janice was just about to make coffee.

FRANK   Funny, when I ask someone in my department
         for a coffee, all I get is a resentful look and no
         sugar. Problem with the young. When I started,
         I saw all demeaning and abusive behaviour as
         a valuable part of my training.

JANICE   Would you like a coffee too, sir?

FRANK   Do you know, I would. Four sugars.

JANICE   Four?

FRANK   Hot and sweet.

JANICE exits. Beat.

ISOBEL   What did you want?

FRANK   Just checking in. How are things?

ISOBEL   Fine.

FRANK   Good.

ISOBEL   Lied.

FRANK   I know. She's angry.

ISOBEL   Maybe that's OK and I have to live with that.

FRANK   Sure. *(Beat)* Sorry I was a bit drunk.

ISOBEL   It's OK.

FRANK   No, you've got enough to be getting on with without me being all loved-up nostalgic.

ISOBEL   It's fine, I'm a big girl.

FRANK   But you must know that if you keep digging around then you are definitely going to throw up some nasty shit.

ISOBEL   Yes, thanks for the metaphor, Frank.

FRANK   It's going to get worse. You OK with that?

ISOBEL   Yes.

FRANK   Right.

ISOBEL   Right.

FRANK   It's not there. I looked.

ISOBEL   What isn't?

FRANK   The fibre.

ISOBEL   You found the box.

FRANK   My world for many years.

ISOBEL   Where was it?

FRANK   It was there.

ISOBEL   No it wasn't. I've been asking them for days.
          They told me—

FRANK   Should have asked me.

ISOBEL   You didn't seem inclined.

FRANK   I'm a friend.

ISOBEL   How could it not be there?

FRANK   I don't know.

ISOBEL   That's a pretty important piece of evidence,
          Frank.

FRANK   From a case twenty-five years old for which
          there have been no appeals in twenty-four.
          It couldn't be more dead.

ISOBEL   Was everything else there?

FRANK   Dunno. Think so.

ISOBEL   So what happened to it?

FRANK   I don't know.

ISOBEL   Fucking hell, Frank, does that not seem
          suspicious to you?

FRANK   No.

ISOBEL   No?

FRANK   It happens.

ISOBEL   Does it – how?

FRANK   It was a few strands in a plastic fucking bag
         – a rogue gust of wind sneaking through a
         corridor could have magicked it away.

ISOBEL   Not buying it.

FRANK   Well maybe you're just too keen to see what
         you want to see.

ISOBEL   That's what he said about us. That fibre put
         him away.

FRANK   No, killing those girls did that.

ISOBEL   And the fibre on him that seemed to match up
         with Sarah McElhenney's coat.

FRANK   Not *seemed* to, Isobel – *did*!

ISOBEL   Can I have it?

FRANK   Have what?

ISOBEL   The box.

FRANK   There's not much in it, just—

ISOBEL   Can I have it?

FRANK   Yes, you can have it.

ISOBEL   When?

FRANK   Whenever you want.

ISOBEL   Can you get hold of Sarah's box too: her
         things?

FRANK   What for?

ISOBEL   I want to see them, Frank. Can you do that?

FRANK   Yes.

ISOBEL   I'm free tomorrow night. Can you bring it to
           me then?

FRANK   Off duty? So it's not a police matter, then?

ISOBEL   Not yet.

FRANK   It's not official?

ISOBEL   Not yet.

FRANK   Filled in the forms?

ISOBEL   No.

FRANK   No form?

ISOBEL   Don't play with me, Frank. *(Beat)* Don't even
           think of saying that thought out loud. Can you
           bring them?

FRANK   OK. The Central bar. Eight o'clock.

ISOBEL   An unsavoury place.

FRANK   Perfect, then, I suppose. Isobel, the mistake
           can easily be made where the fear of your
           future slips doubts into what's been, about
           how you got to now. You need to concentrate on
           what's next for you. The past is an immovable
           object; it's dark and heavy, and the longer you
           look into the darkness, the more your eyes
           seem to see things that aren't there.

ISOBEL   My goodness, Frank, that was pretty poetic for
          a boy from Cardiff's mean streets.

FRANK   You're like a sister.

ISOBEL   Thank you, that's nice.

FRANK   A sister I'd give one to.

ISOBEL   That's not so nice, Frank.

FRANK   It could be.

ISOBEL   What was it you were saying about the past?
          (Beat) Frank, I keep getting a picture of, I
          don't know why, a fox's head. Does that mean
          anything to you?

FRANK   No.

ISOBEL   OK.

    JANICE and DREW enter.

JANICE   Coffee.

FRANK   *(Indicates ISOBEL)* Chief Superintendent
          McArthur could do with both. I'll get on with
          the nasty stuff on the streets.

ISOBEL   I'll have to take this with me.

    ISOBEL exits.

FRANK   Do you think he's attractive?

JANICE   Sir?

FRANK   Prince Harry. How can anyone . . . ?

JANICE   He's mythical. He's a prince. We need that bit
           of glamour.

FRANK   No we don't.

   JANICE exits. DREW lingers.

DREW   How do I get your job?

FRANK   You can't, it's mine.

DREW   I mean, when you're—

FRANK   Dead? Well, you need a bit of that: bit of cold,
           bit of ruthless. You got that?

DREW   I think so.

FRANK   Well, when you know it, let me know and
           we'll talk.

DREW   I have.

FRANK   OK. Thomson's at six. You buy the drinks.

DREW   Anything.

   ISOBEL enters.

ISOBEL   What you two up to?

FRANK   Career guidance.

ISOBEL   Drew, you look suspicious.

DREW   No, ma'am.

FRANK   Well, I'm off.

ISOBEL   Remember the briefing on staffing Thursday.
         You need to get your projections ready or you'll
         lose the argument.

FRANK   I am great at arguing.

ISOBEL   Not what I'm saying.

FRANK   Till tomorrow.

FRANK exits with DREW.

ISOBEL   *(Calls off)* Janice.

JANICE enters.

JANICE   Ma'am?

ISOBEL   When you asked them about the Chalmers
         evidence box, what did they say?

JANICE   Just that they were finding it hard to locate it.

ISOBEL   So it wasn't where it should have been?

JANICE   I don't think it's as straightforward as that. I
         was down in Records for a few weeks, and you
         know the scene in *Raiders of the Lost Ark* at the
         end when you see the warehouse full of crates?

ISOBEL   Really.

JANICE   Various times people have obviously decided
          to improve the filing system, so, depending
          on which year, it depends on which system
          and then it depends on whether someone
          went back and tried to apply the new system
          retrospectively. Or not. If you see what I mean.

ISOBEL   Kind of. Go ask Inspector Ryan to come and
          see me.

JANICE   Any particular reason shall I tell him?

ISOBEL   The trouble with Harry.

JANICE   I think he's sweet.

ISOBEL   Indeed.

JANICE   Ma'am.

JANICE exits.

SCENE THREE

ALEXANDRA enters her home, carrying a camera. She picks up her post. She opens a small package and takes out a USB stick. She sticks it in the computer, pours herself a drink. Whilst she is doing so, the USB has gone to autoplay.

CHALMERS   *(Voice from computer)* Good evening, Alexandra. Listen to the cassettes. Listen to the interview on November the fifth, 1988. Yes, that's Bonfire Night.

MUSIC suddenly plays from the computer. It's 'Teddy Bear's Picnic'.

ALEXANDRA   What the . . . ? Is that all? Come on. Come on.

She goes to the cassettes, rummages till she finds one, puts it on.

CHALMERS   *(Voice from cassette)* You're corrupted, Isobel. I see you in the middle of the road. I can see you and you don't know what to do, what to decide.

ISOBEL   *(Voice from cassette)* I'm always very careful crossing the road. I need to ask you where you were on September the seventeenth, 1988 from seven p.m.—

CHALMERS   *(Voice from cassette)* How much do you trust your colleagues?

FERGUS   *(Voice from cassette)* Where's this going, Alfred?

FRANK   *(Voice from cassette)* You not done the decent thing yet, Chalmers?

CHALMERS   *(Voice from cassette)* If I did, would you be capable of recognising it?

FRANK   *(Voice from cassette)* Clever.

CHALMERS   *(Voice from cassette)* No, that's not clever, at least not to an intelligent man.

ISOBEL   *(Voice from cassette)* Detective Inspector Frank Bowman has entered the room at eleven thirty-four a.m.

FERGUS   *(Voice from cassette)* So tell me about Sarah McElhenney, from 121 Polwarth Gardens.

CHALMERS   *(Voice from cassette)* I've never been there.

FERGUS   *(Voice from cassette)* But you know that's her address?

CHALMERS   *(Voice from cassette)* I don't know anything about her.

ALEXANDRA stops and rewinds the tape.

FERGUS   *(Voice from cassette)* ... Sarah McElhenney, from 121 Polwarth Gardens.

CHALMERS   I've never—

She does it again.

FERGUS   *(Voice from cassette)* ... from 121 Polwarth Gardens.

Stops. Rewinds it again.

FERGUS   *(Voice from cassette)* ... McElhenney, from 121 Polwarth Gardens.

Stops tape. Gets up, moves around.

ALEXANDRA   Fuck. *(Beat)* Fuck fuck fuck. No no no no no. Come on. Fuck. No way. Fuck. Joking. How ... ? Oh no. No.

Laughing off. ISOBEL and FRANK enter. They've had a drink. ISOBEL carries the evidence box.

ISOBEL   I'm afraid your mum has dropped the baton of good and proper behaviour ...

FRANK   It was me! I tripped her up.

ISOBEL   ... but I kind of think it's healthy, y'know, to surprise your children—

ALEXANDRA   Were you never going to tell me?

ISOBEL   About what?

FRANK   You being an alcoholic.

ISOBEL   I'm not an alchol . . . alcoholic.

FRANK   That sounded so bad.

ALEXANDRA   About our house.

ISOBEL   What about our house?

ALEXANDRA walks over to cassette player, rewinds.

ISOBEL   You shouldn't be playing those, Alexandra, it's—

CHALMERS   *(Voice from cassette)* . . . not clever, at least not to an intelligent man.

FERGUS   *(Voice from cassette)* So tell me about Sarah McElhenney, from 121 Polwarth Gardens.

CHALMERS   *(Voice from cassette)* I've never been there.

FERGUS   *(Voice from cassette)* And her?

ALEXANDRA stops the cassette.

ALEXANDRA   That's our address.

ISOBEL   Yes.

ALEXANDRA   That's our home.

ISOBEL   Yes.

ALEXANDRA   Mum?

ISOBEL   I know.

ALEXANDRA   And?

ISOBEL   Please can we talk about this in the
              morning, when I'm—

ALEXANDRA   No! No, we can't do that. We're living in
              Sarah McElhenney's house?

ISOBEL   No, it's our house.

ALEXANDRA   You know what I mean!

ISOBEL   Yes, yes, I do. I'm sorry.

ALEXANDRA   What for?

ISOBEL   Everything you're feeling right now.

ALEXANDRA   You have no idea what I'm feeling right
              now.

ISOBEL   No, I suppose not.

FRANK   Alexandra, you also don't know what it felt
              like back then, not just the investigation,
              the trial, but afterwards, it was—

ALEXANDRA   What was it? How fucked up is that? You
              bought one of the victims' houses. Why?

FRANK backs off.

115

ISOBEL   I don't know.

ALEXANDRA   Why did you do it?

ISOBEL   I don't know.

ALEXANDRA   Of course you know. How could you not know?

ISOBEL   I can't.

ALEXANDRA   Can't what?

ISOBEL   Sorry?

ALEXANDRA   What? What is this? No, Mother, you owe me answers here. I've grown up in a . . . Wait: where?

ISOBEL   What?

ALEXANDRA   Where?

ISOBEL   Darling.

ALEXANDRA   Don't do that.

ISOBEL   Sorry. Things have been stressful. I know.

ALEXANDRA   No you don't.

ISOBEL   And I want you to know that . . .

ALEXANDRA   Oh God, where?

ISOBEL   . . . I never did anything that I believed could ever harm you.

ALEXANDRA   Well you were wrong, Mum, you're—

ISOBEL   I know, I see that – sorry.

ALEXANDRA   Stop saying that stupid useless word.
            Where was she found?

ISOBEL   Oh, Alexandra.

ALEXANDRA   Just tell me. Where?

ISOBEL   I . . .

ALEXANDRA   Oh God, not . . .

ISOBEL   What?

ALEXANDRA   Not in . . . not in my . . .

ISOBEL   No, no, not there.

ALEXANDRA   Right.

ISOBEL   Right. No, no.

ALEXANDRA   Where?

ISOBEL   It was – it was under the floorboards.
            That's where we found her.

ALEXANDRA   Which ones?

ISOBEL   Which ones? Just Sarah.

ALEXANDRA   *Which ones?*

ISOBEL   Oh – I thought you meant which . . . You
            mean the room.

ALEXANDRA   Yes.

ISOBEL   That's good because . . . It was there.

(Beat)

ALEXANDRA   OK.

ISOBEL   I never imagined you would ever know.

ALEXANDRA   What treacheries riddle history with that
            motif.

ISOBEL   *(A little biting)* That from one of your
            projects?

ALEXANDRA   Why, Mum? Why? A dead girl.

ISOBEL   The house was cheap. Her parents needed
            to sell! You weren't even born. It was years
            before . . . *(Beat)* I needed to be close to her,
            maybe. I wasn't coping. I didn't tell anyone
            till after I'd bought . . . I can't explain.

ALEXANDRA   Have you any other secrets? Where does my
            memory of things stop being real?

ISOBEL   You know your own life.

ALEXANDRA   No I don't. I don't.

ISOBEL   For God's sake.

ALEXANDRA   Who is my father?

ISOBEL   Don't ask that! We agreed to never—

ALEXANDRA   And I'm not agreeing any more. Who is he?

ISOBEL   I told you, I—

ALEXANDRA   Is he under the floorboards too? *(Beat)*
Oh my God . . .

ISOBEL   Of course he's not under the floorboards!

ALEXANDRA   Is he under the floorboards, Isobel?

ISOBEL   He's not under the floorboards.

ALEXANDRA   Is my dad . . . What am I saying? OK. I can't
stay here now.

ISOBEL   It was a long time ago.

ALEXANDRA   No. It was today.

ISOBEL   Please.

ALEXANDRA   I can't.

ISOBEL   Oh Alex.

ALEXANDRA   No, I can't. I have to go.

ISOBEL   Don't – you're everything.

ALEXANDRA   No I'm not. And I never have been. So stop
lying.

ISOBEL   I'm sorry.

ALEXANDRA   I'm going.

FRANK   Don't let him do this.

ALEXANDRA   Who?

FRANK   Chalmers – he caused this.

ALEXANDRA   No he didn't.

ISOBEL   You didn't need to know.

ALEXANDRA   Should have kept the lie up?

ISOBEL   There were no lies – I just didn't say.
             For you.

ALEXANDRA   It's ghoulish.

FRANK   When you're dealing with monsters . . .

ALEXANDRA   She's not sure he is a monster. *(To ISOBEL)*
             You know you're not. *(Beat)* So I can also
             tell you now that the project I'm working on
             is with him.

ISOBEL   Who?

ALEXANDRA   Alfred.

FRANK   Alfred? *Alfred?* You're fucking joking.

ALEXANDRA   We made contact months ago, long before
             you came up with your book idea. I saw the
             silver jubilee coming before *you* did! I'm
             going to do a documentary about him.

ISOBEL   You can't.

ALEXANDRA   You can't say that any more.

FRANK   Have you talked with him?

ALEXANDRA   On the phone.

FRANK   What do you think you're doing?

ALEXANDRA   I think I'm getting on with my life.

ISOBEL   This is to get at me, isn't it?

ALEXANDRA   No, this is to get at *me*! Because it seems to me my past isn't what I thought it was at all. Because all the time you were Mum to me and with me, you had *her* in our home, in *you* too. You had a ghost with you and she was part of us and that means, must mean, that we are not what I thought we actually were.

ISOBEL   It's not true.

ALEXANDRA   You don't know what's true. And neither do I.

FRANK   Please stay away from him.

ALEXANDRA   *She* couldn't.

ISOBEL   That's different. I was involved.

ALEXANDRA   And now *I* am. And that's because of you, Mum, don't forget. I'm going to pack now.

ISOBEL   Don't go.

ALEXANDRA   Have to. I can't stay here.

ALEXANDRA exits to her room.

ISOBEL   What do I do?

FRANK   Let her go.

ISOBEL   Just let her go?

FRANK   For now.

ISOBEL   For how long? That's easy for you . . . She can't
         leave.

FRANK   You don't have a choice.

ISOBEL   Of course I do.

FRANK   You're not chief here.

ISOBEL   Oh Frank, what have I done?

FRANK   Well we did all wonder that at the time, when
         you eventually told us, I mean. We knew you
         were struggling.

ISOBEL   You took care of me, you and Fergus. Why did
         I do that? I think I had forgotten. Had I?
         It's a pretty fucked-up thing to do.

FRANK   It *was* a pretty fucked-up thing to do.

ISOBEL   How do I explain that to my daughter?

FRANK   You can't, I think.

ISOBEL   Then what do I do?

FRANK   You have to accept you're not in control.

         ALEXANDRA enters with a bag.

ALEXANDRA   I'm going to Lilly's.

FRANK   I'll get you a cab.

ISOBEL   I could—

ALEXANDRA   I don't want anything from you.

ISOBEL   I'll get you some money, some cash in case
you . . .

ISOBEL exits.

FRANK   Don't let him work on you, Alexandra.
He'll make it confused, then offer you
clarity. Keep away from him. Please.

ALEXANDRA   Why?

FRANK   Why?

ALEXANDRA   Yes, why?

FRANK   He hurts people.

ALEXANDRA   Maybe.

FRANK   Maybe?

ALEXANDRA   Maybe.

FRANK   Your mother helped condemn him. If you
were him, how would you feel about you?

ALEXANDRA   What a mind-bending question.

FRANK   What's on your mind?

ALEXANDRA   What do you mean?

FRANK   Doesn't help: you putting it about.
             The noise.

ALEXANDRA   That's got nothing to do with you. No more
             about that, Frank.

FRANK   What's it about?

ALEXANDRA   Sex.

FRANK   Really?

ALEXANDRA   Women now enjoy sex; it's not like when
             you were young.

FRANK   Your eyes.

ALEXANDRA   You making a move on me now?

FRANK   They're like those pictures of houses or
             villages after a flood.

ALEXANDRA   That's very poetic of you. Mum's been ages.
             Do you think she's having a shit? *(Beat)*
             So you knew.

FRANK   Of course I knew.

ALEXANDRA   Didn't think to say anything? *(Beat)* Know
             what's weird? I think maybe there's nothing
             weird about this at all. That's what's weird.

FRANK   Maybe.

ALEXANDRA   Yes, maybe. Are you my father, Frank?

FRANK   What?

ALEXANDRA   Yes or no.

FRANK   Alex, you—

ALEXANDRA   You see, there's this tide of revelation and
            review in the air and I'm kind of bobbing
            along with its pull, and so it would be good
            to know about any, you know, tidal surges
            or whirlpools I didn't know about.

FRANK   You asked your mum about this?

ALEXANDRA   Because, amazingly, I'm nearly twenty-two
            and I still don't know who my—

FRANK   I know, I—

ALEXANDRA   Are you my fucking father, Frank?

FRANK   No. No, I'm not.

ALEXANDRA   OK, because I'm just trying to get some
            clarity here and I suppose knowing some
            things aren't true is some kind of start.

FRANK   I get it.

ALEXANDRA   I don't! I don't get any of this! I'm in a
            fucking dead person's house. What do you
            think of that?

FRANK   It's unusual.

ALEXANDRA   Frank. That's . . . that's just very true.

FRANK   If you were my daughter I'd be proud, and
                I have always tried to be there, you know,
                if you, if you . . .

ALEXANDRA   I know, Uncle Frank.

FRANK   I don't know who your father is, Alexandra.
                And I know you *think* that's important, but
                I don't. I think the reason he wasn't, is not
                here now, is because he didn't deserve you.

ALEXANDRA   But maybe I should be the one to decide
                that.

FRANK   Yes, maybe.

ALEXANDRA   This is messy.

FRANK   Yes.

ALEXANDRA   Did you ever sleep with her?

FRANK   Yes.

ALEXANDRA   OK. That was straight.

FRANK   But years . . . years before . . .

ALEXANDRA   When?

FRANK   It wasn't for long: round about the time
                of . . .

ALEXANDRA   Chalmers.

FRANK   Chalmers, yeah.

ALEXANDRA   God, he gets everywhere, doesn't he?

FRANK   I think the experience was tough on your
        mum. She went on a bit of a run.

ALEXANDRA   Bit of a run?

FRANK   Yeah, men, you know.

ALEXANDRA   Ugh. Naughty Mum.

FRANK   I don't think she was enjoying it as such.

ALEXANDRA   What a shame. I think I'm a bit scared,
            Uncle Frank.

FRANK   That's good, Alexandra.

*ISOBEL enters. It's clear she's been crying. She hands
ALEXANDRA some money.*

ISOBEL   You don't need to go.

ALEXANDRA   I do.

ISOBEL   Don't go.

ALEXANDRA   I'm going.

ISOBEL   Leave Alfred Chalmers to me.

ALEXANDRA   You want all the glory.

ISOBEL   There's no glory to get.

ALEXANDRA   Everything keeps being dragged back to
            then, to that time, doesn't it? *(Beat)* It's like
            a black hole. Even our home is not what it

was. Or maybe for you it's not a dark hole
at all. It's the light.

ISOBEL   I love you.

ALEXANDRA   *(Crying)* What did you do, Mum? What did
              you do?

ALEXANDRA leaves.

FRANK   I'll take her . . . Are you OK?

ISOBEL   I'm fine. Go.

FRANK   I could stay . . .

ISOBEL   No, go. Please go.

*FRANK exits. ISOBEL sits, opens Sarah's file. She takes out
a purse. A bracelet. Ring. She looks in the purse, takes out
some coins, notes. She opens a bit of the purse and takes
out receipts, three or four bus tickets.*

ISOBEL   Did you collect bus tickets, Sarah? These
              are May, May, May, June – a whole three
              months before he took you. The 23. She took
              your bus route to university, Alexandra.
              She rode on your bus. Where did you go to,
              I wonder? Receipts: April, sandwich and a
              coffee; May, bowl of soup, a Marathon;
              May, sandwich and crisps. Student Union?
              You ate at the university. But you had a
              benefit card?

She checks all three receipts.

ISOBEL   You weren't really unemployed, were you,
          Sarah? You were a student. So why did no
          one . . . ? Because. Oh stupid stupid. Who
          wants their dead daughter's name in the
          papers for benefit fraud? You broke the
          pattern, Sarah. You weren't like the others.
          And we missed it.

SCENE FOUR

CHALMERS in the waiting room. He is nervous, tap-tapping.
JUDITH is there.

CHALMERS   Is that the right time?

JUDITH   Yes, Alfred . . .

ISOBEL is late. Finally she arrives.

CHALMERS   You're late. I can't abide it when—

ISOBEL   You've been in contact with my daughter.

CHALMERS   Oh. Yes, I have. Sorry.

ISOBEL   Sorry?

CHALMERS   What can I say?

ISOBEL   Well, what can *I* say?

ISOBEL gets up to leave.

CHALMERS   Wait. How was I to know you would turn up?

ISOBEL   You made contact with my daughter?

CHALMERS   It was an accident.

ISOBEL   Liar.

CHALMERS   You put me in here!

ISOBEL   Not interested. It's finished.

CHALMERS   I was going to string her along, probably
            let her do her documentary, feed her a few
            scraps. It gets publicity. Maybe it gets my
            case looked at! Shames you. Maybe messes
            up you and her just like you did to me.
            Revenge on you and yours. A bit nasty, but
            nothing compared to what you did to me!

ISOBEL   Oh, I don't know.

CHALMERS   What don't you know?

ISOBEL   Where it begins and ends with you, the
            truth, the lies; never did.

CHALMERS   What do you think I could have done,
            Isobel? I'm here! I'm an old man.

ISOBEL   I don't know.

CHALMERS   There's nothing else to know.

ISOBEL   I need some time.

CHALMERS   My time is on your hands, missy.

ISOBEL   And what's on yours?

CHALMERS   Less than you think.

ISOBEL   I don't think so.

CHALMERS   But you're not sure.

ISOBEL   No.

CHALMERS Do you know something? *(Beat)* Suspect?
          Smell? Taste? An itch you can't get rid of?

ISOBEL   There's evidence missing. The fibre.

CHALMERS Missing? How could that happen?

ISOBEL   I don't know.

CHALMERS But what do you think?

ISOBEL   It could just have happened.

CHALMERS Just happened? Chief Superintendent?
          Just happened.

ISOBEL   Happens.

CHALMERS Does it?

ISOBEL   I was going to have it checked. Forensics
          has moved on.

CHALMERS But now?

ISOBEL   Now I can't.

CHALMERS Who knows you were talking to me?

ISOBEL   I told Black Fergus and Frank.

CHALMERS Anyone else?

ISOBEL   No one. They were angry. They didn't
          understand.

CHALMERS Oh, they understood.

ISOBEL   Fergus has had a stroke. I thought *I* caused
          it. But then . . .

CHALMERS But then? Then you thought—

ISOBEL   I thought, what if it was guilt?

CHALMERS I know about guilt, Isobel. I've always felt
          guilty, but not like you might think. Guilty
          that I was me. That I was who I was. I was
          cleverer than any of them but I could not
          make sense of why . . . why no one could
          find a way to like me. I was amazed when
          my wife agreed to accompany me to the
          pictures, then to dinner, took me to meet
          her parents. And then when she married me
          and had my daughter, I always felt like I'd
          be found out and they'd see I wasn't worth
          it. But I didn't deserve to lose them like
          I did. So when they abandoned me, as of
          course they would, that guilt was like I was
          burning. Not because of murder. But guilt at
          the inevitable misery of drawing them close
          to me and making them suffer.

ISOBEL   Your daughter never made contact?

CHALMERS I suppose she must have read the
          headlines. Seen the pictures of me dressed
          in guilt – handcuffs and hoods. And then
          the pictures of those girls.

ISOBEL   The girls.

CHALMERS   I want to help you.

ISOBEL   Good.

CHALMERS   I want to help you get what you need.

ISOBEL   OK.

CHALMERS   That fourth victim.

ISOBEL   Yes?

CHALMERS   The one you nailed me on.

ISOBEL   Yes, I know.

CHALMERS   The other three just sat under the trial but with no evidence.

ISOBEL   You had no alibis.

CHALMERS   I'm not on trial again here. I'm trying to give you something, girl, so listen.

ISOBEL   Go ahead.

CHALMERS   Was there any connection with someone on the case – besides yourself – who might be seen to benefit from the death of that girl and my conviction?

ISOBEL   Well – I always knew it had helped my career.

CHALMERS   Just you?

ISOBEL   Fergus was made chief constable, but . . .

CHALMERS   But? And Frank? You don't have the answer
            because you've not done the thinking, so
            you need to go now and think. But you
            smell it, don't you? You know you got it
            wrong. I think you probably smelled it then.
            I think you did, didn't you?

ISOBEL   I thought you did it.

CHALMERS   And that's where it all went wrong and
            when the smell started.

ISOBEL   No alibis. It was you. We all sat and looked
            at the facts and it was you. All the girls had
            their abortions in your ward.

CHALMERS   And now?

ISOBEL   It was you.

CHALMERS   Why would I waste my time with a lie?
            Think. I want the sun. I also have a
            daughter somewhere out there cursed
            with what you, Black Fergus and Frank
            Bowman did to her. Something went wrong
            that night you arrested me, or before then.
            Halloween. Remember. Think back, and if
            you didn't do something, someone else did.

ISOBEL gets up to go.

ISOBEL   She was a student. The fourth girl. All the
                other three were unemployed. She was
                different.

CHALMERS   *(Beat)* Was she?

ISOBEL   And what was the fox doing?

CHALMERS   The fox again?

ISOBEL   There was a fox. When he – you – took her
                eyes.

CHALMERS   What's a fox got to do with this?

ISOBEL   Don't know.

CHALMERS   Hold your nerve. Get the truth out before it
                rots you. Get the truth and write your book
                and I promise I'll leave Alexandra alone,
                never speak to her again. I'll refuse.

ISOBEL   I could stop that anyway.

CHALMERS   Could you? Youth, you know.

JUDITH   Time's up.

ISOBEL   I don't want you ever contacting her again.

CHALMERS   Of course. Isobel. Thank you. Don't feel
                guilty. Don't hate. Look where it got me.

*ISOBEL exits. Voices off. CHALMERS sits for a while. He
gets up and exits, JUDITH opening the door for him.*

SCENE FIVE

ISOBEL enters. Drunk. Maybe with chips. Perhaps a sound of something as she enters. She tries to put the light on but it doesn't work. Tries several times. It is very dark and shadowy.

ISOBEL   Thanks. Thanks for that.

The answerphone light is flashing. She goes over, manages to press the right button.

ALEXANDRA   *(Voice from the answerphone)* OK, Mum, so you've managed to mess that up for me too. Tried calling him at the time we agreed but he was 'not available'. Got a message saying it was best we didn't 'proceed with our project'. My project. So you win. Well done you. Like always, Chief Superintendent McArthur. I'd say I hate you but then I'd sound like a teenager and I'd feel even more stupid, ridiculous and failing than I already do. I don't know what age I am any more. I'm thinking of leaving uni.

The dead tone tells us she has hung up.

ISOBEL   Good. Good.

Suddenly a person in a fox-head mask appears and attacks
ISOBEL, hitting her several times with something, probably
from the house. As ISOBEL lies still, groaning, the person
grabs some of the files, photos, etc., and stuffs them into
a holdall. ISOBEL crawls across the floor. She manages to
get her hands on her mobile and starts dialling. FOXHEAD
sees her, takes the phone from her, smashes it, pulls out
the house phone from the socket. Looks as if there might
be more violence visited on ISOBEL, but then FOXHEAD
exits quickly. ISOBEL recovers, manages to drag herself up
to the settee.

ISOBEL   What am I doing? What have I done? *(She*
          screams, more in anger than anything else) Piece
          it together. Piece it together, Isobel. Man up!
          Come on. Man up! He comes here, gets in – or
          does he come in with her? – and kills her; he
          scrapes her eyes out, pours in the tar, puts the
          diamanté in but he doesn't place her in his
          constellation. You didn't do that.

CHALMERS appears or enters in the shadows, half seen.

ISOBEL   Where are you?

CHALMERS Always where you want me to be. I'm in
          your house.

ISOBEL   Why did you leave her here?

CHALMERS   That'd be telling.

ISOBEL   Why did you hide her?

CHALMERS   Because she wasn't for showing.

ISOBEL   Not like the others.

CHALMERS   Didn't know that till after.

ISOBEL   Of course you didn't.

CHALMERS   What if I tell you I didn't do them all?

ISOBEL   Two killers?

CHALMERS   And I wasn't either of them.

ISOBEL   It had to be you. Alfred, the stars have all died out now. It's time to be honest. Did you kill her? Did you kill all those girls?

CHALMERS   Listen, just because this is your projection doesn't mean I'm still not cleverer than you are.

ISOBEL   Doesn't make sense and is impossible. Why bury her in her own house?

CHALMERS   Why not? Moving a body around can be difficult.

ISOBEL   You didn't want her to be found? No, you hid her. You were ashamed?

CHALMERS   You sent me down on an illusion. You
            worked it up between you, loved-up group
            of liars.

ISOBEL   It wasn't a stitch-up.

CHALMERS   Your drive is your weakness. When it heard
            the crowd cheering, it just went for it. You
            went for me. You got me.

ISOBEL   The fibres proved it.

CHALMERS   Oh, you mean the fibres that have gone
            walkies?

ISOBEL   *(Holding her arm and groaning)* I feel sick.

CHALMERS   Even now you give me indigestion on
            a meal I ate twenty-five years ago.

ISOBEL   You can't invent forensic evidence.

CHALMERS   No, but you can put it where it never
            should have been.

ISOBEL   Why?

CHALMERS   The story was too good not to be true.
            So you, or maybe Black Fergus or your
            boyfriend, Frank, made sure the narrative
            stuck.

ISOBEL   They're good cops. And he's not my
            boyfriend.

CHALMERS   A good cop doesn't create fictions, only facts.
            But you were too hungry.

ISOBEL   I wanted to stop the murders. They were
              alive when you took out their eyes!

CHALMERS   And hungry for Frank too – yes, gobbled
              him up just like you gob—

He spits out an eyeball that he has eaten.

CHALMERS   That's disgusting.

ISOBEL   I didn't mean that.

CHALMERS   Then why is it here? You're getting off on
              this too much.

ISOBEL   I only want the truth.

CHALMERS   Like I'm a piece of porn. A piece of porn you
              made. And maybe thought you shouldn't
              have. But love to watch.

ISOBEL   What's the fox head?

CHALMERS   The head of an animal.

ISOBEL   You've told me nothing.

CHALMERS   I've told you truths. Now excuse me whilst
              I enjoy the illusion of freedom in my past.

There is a sound off, like a door opening and closing.

CHALMERS   Her. Sarah. She's come home.

ISOBEL   No.

SARAH McELHENNEY enters the room. Sees CHALMERS, who lunges at her. It is a terrible murder, messy and violent.

CHALMERS   Why are you making me do this?

ISOBEL   I'm not making you do it. Stop!

CHALMERS   It's already done!

SARAH   Jesus Christ, why did you let him do this?

ISOBEL   We tried to catch him! I'm sorry!

CHALMERS   You waste-of-space whore, cutting out life when you've no value. There's no light in you, none at all!

SARAH   You bitch, my mother's watching this.

ISOBEL   No she's not.

SARAH   She's always watching this.

ISOBEL   I want it to stop.

SARAH   How do you think I feel?

CHALMERS   I didn't do this!

He finds several bus tickets and a student card in his hand.

CHALMERS   You're a student. But that's wrong.

ALEXANDRA walks in wearing provocative nightwear. She's horrified at the visioning her mother is doing.

ISOBEL   Dressed like a slut as usual!

ALEXANDRA   What is wrong with you?

ISOBEL   Alexandra, get out.

ALEXANDRA   *(Indicating murder)* What is all that about?

ISOBEL   I'm trying to find the thing that just lets me
            understand the—

ALEXANDRA   Well, I'm trying to have sex, if you don't
            mind. Oooooh, I feel weirdly horny. I'm
            finding this a wee bit of a turn-on. Is that
            wrong?

*FOXHEAD appears again at window. ALEXANDRA goes to
exit. CHALMERS sees her for the first time. They both stare
at each other for a long moment.*

CHALMERS   Sarah?

ALEXANDRA   Alexandra.

CHALMERS   I've made a terrible mistake.

ISOBEL   What mistake?

CHALMERS   I don't make mistakes.

ALEXANDRA   Is she dead?

CHALMERS   She doesn't fit into the sky.

ISOBEL   Doesn't she?

CHALMERS   I broke the truth of it. There's no pattern –
            no meaning.

ISOBEL   But then?

CHALMERS   *(To ALEXANDRA)* Sarah?

ALEXANDRA   I'm Alexandra.

CHALMERS   *(Indicates SARAH)* She's a student.

ALEXANDRA   Is she?

SARAH   Yes.

ALEXANDRA   Shouldn't you be dead by now?

CHALMERS   In a bit. *(Still to ALEXANDRA)* Sarah?

ISOBEL   Stop talking to her. She's my daughter.

ALEXANDRA   I was just having sex and I heard all this.

CHALMERS   I made a mistake. She's a student.

ALEXANDRA   I'm a student. We took the same bus, didn't
            we, Mum?

CHALMERS   You're a student too?

ALEXANDRA   Yes.

CHALMERS   Two of you. *(To SARAH)* Sarah? Sarah?
            (Beat) She's dead now. Look what you made
            me do.

ISOBEL   You must have done it.

CHALMERS   Did I?

ALEXANDRA   It's OK, we'll work it out.

ISOBEL   Stay away from him, Alexandra.

ALEXANDRA moves physically a little closer to CHALMERS.

ISOBEL   Oh please, my darling daughter. Oh please,
Alexandra.

FOXHEAD appears in room.

ALEXANDRA   Aren't you going to make a constellation
with her?

CHALMERS   She's only one. You can't make a
constellation with only one star.

ALEXANDRA   That's true, Mum. Even I know that.

CHALMERS   You need two.

ISOBEL   I'm really really sorry and I love you.

*FOXHEAD runs up to ALEXANDRA and places a knife at her
throat, stays there panting for a while.*

CHALMERS   This has nothing to do with me.

*CHALMERS exits, dragging SARAH's body off. As soon as
he has gone, FOXHEAD suddenly disengages and runs off.
ALEXANDRA remains still.*

ISOBEL   Are you all right?

*ALEXANDRA picks a hair from her clothing where FOXHEAD
had its face.*

ALEXANDRA   Yes. Yes. I'd better go and finish the sex off
             now.

ISOBEL   You go and finish your sex off, my darling.

ALEXANDRA   OK, Mum.

ALEXANDRA exits.

ISOBEL   Facts. Facts, Isobel, facts. Four murders. Three
             unemployed women who'd had abortions.
             A student who'd had an abortion. Three
             displayed in a constellation, the other hidden.
             All four, tar-filled eyes and diamanté. A trick of
             yours to put us off? Or you made a mistake. Or
             was there a copycat who wanted to frame you?
             Or are you the fall guy and I drove it home
             because of bad maths? And you're innocent?
             And the fucking fox . . . ? *(Groans)* I'm trying,
             Sarah. I'm getting nearer. Stay with me.
             Oh dear God, I'm trying to see. I'm open to
             everything.

Blackout with ISOBEL sitting there.

SCENE SIX

FRANK and FERGUS in ISOBEL's office. Waiting. FERGUS in a wheelchair. His speech is impaired from his stroke.

FERGUS   Are you sure she is due in?

FRANK   Yes. Young Drew told me.

FERGUS   Everyone is young now.

FRANK   Right.

FERGUS   Apart from me.

FRANK   Right.

FERGUS   Do you think the stroke was a signal that old age is near?

FRANK   Fergus, the train passed that signal a wee while back!

FERGUS   Fuck . . . Do you love her?

FRANK   Probably. As much as I know what that bollocks means.

FERGUS   You just know it.

FRANK   OK then. *(Beat)* Fergus, don't take this wrong, but you talking about love with me . . . Let's stick to whisky, golf and crime, eh?

FERGUS All right.

FRANK Hope you don't mind.

FERGUS Fuck you.

FRANK Thanks.

FERGUS Okey-dokey.

ISOBEL enters. Her arm is in a sling.

ISOBEL Frank? Fergus?

FRANK What happened to your arm?

ISOBEL Fell off my bike.

FRANK Didn't tell me.

ISOBEL Should I have?

DREW enters.

DREW The minister's special adviser is here.

ISOBEL Is she? How did you and Detective Superintendent Bowman get on in the pub the other night?

DREW Fine, ma'am.

ISOBEL That's good then, Drew, that's good.

DREW What will I tell her?

ISOBEL Say I'll be right there.

DREW   How long?

FRANK   Just do it, son.

DREW exits.

ISOBEL   Where were you last Thursday night?

FRANK   What?

ISOBEL   Where were you?

FRANK   I don't know. At home, probably. Though not
         a Champions League night, so frankly could
         have been anywhere.

ISOBEL   Right.

FRANK   Why?

ISOBEL   Just wondered.

FRANK   Oh really.

ISOBEL   I just wondered. *(With sudden briskness)* I need
         to get ready.

FERGUS   Say what you are thinking.

ISOBEL   Got the minister breathing down my neck.
         I'd better go.

FERGUS   What do you think of Frank?

ISOBEL   What does that mean?

FRANK   Yeah, what does—

FERGUS   Do you think he's a liar?

FRANK   Fuck's sake, Fergus.

FERGUS   What do you think he did? What's he covering up, Isobel?

ISOBEL   I'm making connections, but I don't know if they're real.

FERGUS   Then ask the questions.

ISOBEL   I don't know if I know what the questions are.

DREW re-enters.

DREW   That's them here, how—

ISOBEL   Five minutes.

DREW   Will I say—

ISOBEL   You'll say five fucking minutes, that's what you'll say.

DREW   Will do, ma'am.

DREW exits.

ISOBEL   I try to imagine how it was with . . . with the women who were killed.

FRANK   I thought you'd stopped doing that *Cracker* thing.

ISOBEL   And I keep seeing this . . . It's like a man in
          a fox's head, all bloody and terrible.

FRANK   This is something you imagined, yeah?

ISOBEL   You used to say my imagination and logic were
          friends when for most people they are enemies.

FRANK   I used to suck on my mother's nipples too, but
          not now!

ISOBEL   Frank, that is disgusting.

FRANK   I know, I don't know why I said that.

ISOBEL   You were making a point.

FRANK   I *was* making a point.

ISOBEL   It's OK.

FRANK   Is it?

FERGUS   All over again.

ISOBEL   What, Fergus?

FERGUS   Him. All over again. It's what he does.
          He's doing it again.

ISOBEL   Are you, either of you, hiding something from
          me? Is there something you have done that you
          don't want me to know?

FERGUS and FRANK hesitate.

ISOBEL   Oh God.

FERGUS   Don't think the worst.

ISOBEL   I was attacked Thursday night.

FRANK   Didn't know.

ISOBEL   Nobody knows. I wasn't at work. It was in my home.

FRANK   How—

ISOBEL   Don't know. I was drunk. I've been leaving the latch open just in case Alexandra . . . Only the person that attacked me had on a mask. A fox head. Not something I imagined. Real. Which is interesting because there are only two people I have mentioned this to and that is you, Frank, and Alfred Chalmers.

FRANK   You think I attacked you?

ISOBEL   Maybe not you. *(Looks in direction of the door)* I don't know.

FRANK   Yes you do.

ISOBEL   I don't.

FRANK   OK, fuck this. I'm a good man, Isobel.

ISOBEL   What did that good man do?

FRANK   I do the right thing. He did it. He killed those women.

ISOBEL   You know that?

FRANK   I'm saying those girls aren't here to speak for
          themselves now.

ISOBEL   And you speak for them, do you?

FRANK   Who do you speak for? For him? I am a messy
          human being in a very messy fucked-up planet
          and here is the thing I know best: that when
          I meet my God, I can look him in the face and
          say I tried to make the shit a little better by
          what I did. And I tell you, Isobel, I call it now
          and I say he's guilty and those girls were
          denied a life of love and mess because he cut
          them off. Good luck with your indulgent search
          for the truth.

   FRANK starts to leave.

ISOBEL   You can't just walk away from this.

FRANK   This is as close to self-harming in police work
          as I've ever seen!

ISOBEL   Someone attacked me!

FERGUS   Tell her. *(FRANK stops)* Tell her.

FRANK   Fergus!

ISOBEL   Tell me what?

   FRANK is silent.

FERGUS   It was a Wolfman . . .

ISOBEL   A what?

FERGUS   The night we arrested him. It was Halloween, remember. The station had a party. And we all had masks on.

ISOBEL   Did we?

FERGUS   We did.

ISOBEL   Oh my God. Did the fabric from one of the masks . . .

FRANK   Maybe. *Maybe.*

ISOBEL   What? It matched the fabric from her – Sarah's fur coat?

FRANK   That's not the point!

ISOBEL   Did someone put it on his jacket? And now that someone has decided to get rid of the evidence just in case a new forensics test would be damning.

FRANK   No.

ISOBEL   Well who did then, Frank? Who put the fucking mask on Chalmers' jacket?

FERGUS   You did.

Silence.

ISOBEL   What?

FRANK   Jesus, Fergus.

FERGUS   You did.

ISOBEL   No, no. *(Beat)* No. *(Beat)* I can't . . .

FERGUS   It was you, Isobel.

FRANK   You put the mask on the mannequin. The
             mannequin had Chalmers' jacket on it. Waiting
             to be taken to Forensics. In a couple of hours it
             wouldn't have been there. It would have been
             in a lab. And then, yes, maybe history would
             have turned out differently. It was a moment,
             only a moment. The beast's head on the body of
             the beast. You laughed. And then we laughed.
             We were all drunk, elated and destroyed all
             at the same time and came in to look at him
             on the CCTV and feel good that no young
             woman out there would die that night. It was
             Halloween. And we had masks. And you were
             the Wolfman.

ISOBEL   No, no, I would remember that.

FRANK   I don't think it even occurred to us, to put the
             two together at the time.

ISOBEL   It didn't *occur*? Why can't I remember that?
             Why can't I remember what happened? What's
             wrong with me?

FERGUS   We care for you. And we were right to care for you.

ISOBEL   He needs to be freed.

FERGUS   Chalmers is a murderer.

ISOBEL   No, this confirms—

FRANK   Nothing. That fibre might not have come from the Wolfman mask. It might have been Sarah's coat.

ISOBEL   But we don't know that.

FRANK   It is possible.

ISOBEL   That's not our job.

FRANK   Kill the conversations with Chalmers, Isobel. Has Alexandra cut off from him?

ISOBEL   I've ended that. He just wants me. He thinks I can give him justice. Can I?

FRANK   That's been done.

ISOBEL   The only real evidence was a lie.

FRANK   Was *maybe* a lie.

ISOBEL   It was me.

FRANK   I've been doing a bit of work. I found out how he contacted Alexandra. It was fucking Twitter.

ISOBEL   But he can't have—

FRANK   But he has. So it looks like he's got a
          smartphone or access to a computer.

ISOBEL   Did you get rid of that strand of fibre?

FRANK   If I say no, will you believe me? If I say I did it.
          For you. Where would that leave you?

ISOBEL   That's not what we do. We just take the
          evidence and we act.

FRANK   We're here to get the bad guys. Whatever crisis
          is storming your sense of right and wrong, you
          need to get over it fast, or have you forgotten
          how much of a monster he is? You can't *change*
          that. You can't reinvent that.

FERGUS   Have I been struck down by God, Isobel?

ISOBEL   No, Fergus.

FERGUS   In my blacker Black Fergus moments, I don't
          know.

ISOBEL   You're a good man.

FERGUS   How do you know?

ISOBEL   Because I know.

FERGUS   Call Chalmers now, because you know it is the
          right thing. Because you *know*.

ISOBEL   Do I?

They sit in silence. She picks up her mobile and calls.

ISOBEL   Hello, Judith? *(Beat)* This is Isobel McArthur.
         (Beat) Yes, I wonder if you could relay a simple
         message to Alfred Chalmers. *(Beat)* Thanks.
         It is: 'There will be no more meetings. There
         will be no book. Nothing has changed.' *(Beat)*
         Yes, thank you. Bye.

FERGUS   Excellent access facilities here.

FRANK wheels FERGUS out.

ISOBEL   *(Calls off)* Janice?

JANICE enters.

JANICE   Ma'am?

ISOBEL   Get the tea and biscuits out. I'm ready.

JANICE   Will do.

ISOBEL sits in her chair and waits.

SCENE SEVEN

CHALMERS   So dark and only four o'clock. Where's Judith today?

MALE NURSE   Called in sick.

CHALMERS   Nothing serious, I hope?

The YOUNG MALE NURSE exits. CHALMERS feels about underneath the table, finds something and is satisfied. The door of the waiting room opens and the YOUNG MALE NURSE enters with, following him, ALEXANDRA. CHALMERS is visibly excited.

CHALMERS   I never imagined . . . You are really here.

ALEXANDRA   Yes. Here I am.

CHALMERS   I know you must be nervous, but please relax. You are the first new, sane person I have met for over twenty-five years who didn't want to either contain or medicate me.

ALEXANDRA   I don't want to do either of those things.

CHALMERS   No, I know. I'm a little overwhelmed that this has happened. I'm sorry if I let you down, Alexandra, but your mother's book could have seen me get justice and freedom.

ALEXANDRA   I understand, but I needed to see you. How did you get your granddaughter's passport?

CHALMERS   It's not real. I have found some rare advantages to my current society and their less than savoury networks and skills.

ALEXANDRA   They wouldn't let me bring the recorder in.

CHALMERS   Need to plan for that. Papers, et cetera, et cetera.

ALEXANDRA   I feel I can look at you, and I know you can't be guilty.

CHALMERS   How does that feel?

ALEXANDRA   It makes me feel it was right to come here.

CHALMERS   I think it was. How is your mother about this?

ALEXANDRA   She doesn't know.

CHALMERS   Ah.

ALEXANDRA   She asked me to stop the contact.

CHALMERS   And why didn't you?

ALEXANDRA   Because I think there's something stuck back then for me too, like something lodged in the back of my throat. This could just sort things maybe for all three of us.

CHALMERS   Well . . .

ALEXANDRA   Listen, Alfred, I don't want to put pressure
             on you, but *this* is the thing that's getting
             me through right now.

CHALMERS   Don't worry, what we're going to do will
             give you all the profile you need.

ALEXANDRA   And help you.

CHALMERS   And help me.

ALEXANDRA   Can't believe they didn't let me bring the
             recorder in.

CHALMERS   To see you so upset over a thing like that.

ALEXANDRA   Sorry, was that insensitive?

CHALMERS   No, but it reminds me of what freedom is.

ALEXANDRA   That's beautiful. Do you mind if I write that
             down?

CHALMERS   No, no – go ahead.

ALEXANDRA   *(Getting her notepad out)* I think what I want
             to do is start from your words, next time
             I come, maybe. Then I'll, like, visit where
             you grew up, where you lived at the time …
             when you were arrested. Take some footage.
             But then I just want to listen to your words
             and see what pictures and music come to
             me so that it's not literal but poetic, so we
             create something where truth lives behind
             the eyes of facts. Does that sound OK,
             Alfred?

CHALMERS   It sounds powerful.

ALEXANDRA   It could be.

CHALMERS   It will need to be. You're probably my last
            chance. I never felt I had completed my
            statement of life, if you like.

ALEXANDRA   When I found out where . . . where I was
            living, I felt like *my* past was a lie.

CHALMERS   It was a mistake.

ALEXANDRA   No, it wasn't – how can you make a mistake
            like buying the house of the murder victim
            you were investigating?

CHALMERS   No, I mean I shouldn't have killed her. It
            was a mistake. She was a whore, but she
            hadn't one foot in the gutter.

ALEXANDRA   You did it?

CHALMERS   Oh yes.

ALEXANDRA   But . . .

CHALMERS   I know, I know . . .

*CHALMERS suddenly starts to choke. He doubles over
the table.*

CHALMERS   Nurse. Nurse.

*The **YOUNG MALE NURSE** rushes over to help him. In a second, Chalmers has him over the table and sticks a knife he procures from under the table into him. The **NURSE** slides to the floor. **CHALMERS** takes his keys from out of his pocket and locks the door, keeping the key in the lock.*

CHALMERS   Do you have a fag?

ALEXANDRA   A what?

CHALMERS   A fucking fag, bitch, are you thick?

ALEXANDRA   I don't smoke.

CHALMERS   Fuck, doesn't smoke! Well, what will you and I talk about now?

SCENE EIGHT

ISOBEL's living room is empty. ISOBEL enters and puts the lights on. She's on the phone. There is a real and bloody head of a fox in the living room. ISOBEL doesn't notice.

ISOBEL   . . . Please, Alexandra, just call. Love you.

She takes off her hat, maybe fires up the laptop. Finally she sees what we have all seen. She stops. At that moment a figure in a mask comes through the hallway door. ISOBEL makes to escape but the person pulls out a gun and points it at her.

ISOBEL   Who are you and what do you want? *(Beat)* Frank? Drew? Just take what you want and go.

The person takes off the mask. It is JUDITH, the young female nurse.

ISOBEL   You?

JUDITH   Sit down. Sit down!

ISOBEL does so.

ISOBEL   What now?

JUDITH   You'll see. Just wait.

ISOBEL   Is someone else coming?

JUDITH   Shut up.

ISOBEL   If you—

JUDITH   Shut up! Stop talking. I don't want you to talk.

ISOBEL   OK.

JUDITH takes out a mobile phone, texts and holds it in her hand. Waits.

ISOBEL   Whatever he told you, it's not true.

JUDITH   I know everything.

ISOBEL   He's manipulated you.

JUDITH   No, he's manipulated you. Silly cow.

ISOBEL   He manipulates everybody.

JUDITH   You're funny.

ISOBEL   I'm sorry if—

JUDITH   You should be sorry. He shouldn't be there.

ISOBEL   Oh yes he should.

JUDITH   *(As in panto)* Oh no he shouldn't. *(Beat)* You didn't get him. You cheated. You're a liar and a cheat. He had a family and—

ISOBEL   And Sarah McElhenney didn't?

JUDITH   He's a visionary. He had things to say.

ISOBEL   What were those things?

JUDITH   *(Remembering his words)* That we squander the life that's given us. That we abuse it. Make it empty. And then there's nothing. He needed us to wake up, to look up.

ISOBEL   There must be something wrong with the screening procedure at the unit. You're vulnerable.

JUDITH   *You're* vulnerable! I killed that fox. It's not easy to find a fox. You see them sometimes in the city. But when you want to kill one, it's not easy. Even the foxes don't know where they should be. They don't even know what they are any more. It's a mess. Never killed anything before. Had to keep it in my fridge. Yuck. Let me tell you, I've had to eat tinned food for the past five days. Still, worth it, though. You should have seen your face. *(Laughs)*

CHALMERS in the meeting room has taken out a phone and dialled.

ISOBEL   It's not too late to—

JUDITH's phone rings.

ISOBEL   Who's that?

JUDITH   You'll see. *(Answers)* Hello, Alfred.

CHALMERS   Hello, Judith. How are things your side?

JUDITH   They're fine.

CHALMERS   Good. Good.

JUDITH   Stay still!

ALEXANDRA   Who are you—

CHALMERS   Did I say you could speak?

JUDITH   Stop moving! Yours?

CHALMERS   All is well. *(To ALEXANDRA)* My colleague
has someone there for you if you want to
say a few words.

ALEXANDRA   Who?

CHALMERS   Put the phone on speaker now.

JUDITH   OK.

CHALMERS   It's your mum, Alexandra.

The phone speakers are both on now.

ALEXANDRA   Mum?

ISOBEL   Alexandra!

ALEXANDRA   Mum, he's killed a nurse and he's locked us
in the room.

CHALMERS   That's enough.

ISOBEL   Alexandra, just do what he says. It'll be fine.

JUDITH   No it won't!

CHALMERS   Keep calm, Judith.

JUDITH   But she's—

CHALMERS   Stop getting excitable.

JUDITH   We've waited so long, Alfred, it's—

CHALMERS   Quiet! Isobel?

ISOBEL   Yes.

CHALMERS   It's good to meet your daughter. I hear she's
            moved out.

ISOBEL   Yes.

CHALMERS   No loyalty, eh?

ISOBEL   She's brilliant. She's becoming her own
            person.

CHALMERS   No, Isobel, you fucked up again. Just like
            you did all those years ago when you set
            me up.

ISOBEL   But you killed her.

CHALMERS   I know I killed her. I killed them all, of
            course I did that, but you didn't catch me.

ISOBEL   Then why are you there?

CHALMERS   Because of an injustice. Because of an
            ambitious young woman. I'm a bit flattered,
            though. I mean, to buy little Sarah's flat.
            No wonder your daughter's so needy.
            (To ALEXANDRA) Aren't you? Aren't you, girl?

ALEXANDRA   *(Crying)* Yes.

CHALMERS   Go on, say it.

ALEXANDRA   I'm needy.

CHALMERS   Again.

ALEXANDRA   I'm needy.

CHALMERS   Again.

ALEXANDRA   I'm needy.

ISOBEL   Please stop this, Alfred, there is nothing
            you can gain from it.

CHALMERS   That's not true.

ISOBEL   What can you gain that means anything?

CHALMERS   There isn't anything that means anything.

ISOBEL   It's not about the girls, it never was. This is
            about you. About you trying to give yourself
            meaning, isn't it? It's you that's needy, not
            my daughter.

CHALMERS   That's enough of your talking now, 'cause
            it's my turn and you don't spoil it for me!
            But you know, Isobel, for a little while I

thought you might actually get me out.
It did make me break my stride for a bit
on the Alexandra project.

ISOBEL   Please don't harm her. It's me you need to
take revenge on.

CHALMERS   Judith?

JUDITH   Yes.

CHALMERS   Shoot her.

JUDITH shoots ISOBEL in the leg.

ALEXANDRA   Mum. Don't kill my mum, please.

ISOBEL   It's OK, Alexandra. I'm OK.

ALEXANDRA   Mum!

CHALMERS   Already this feels better. Something real
is happening. And the good thing is that
probably no one will even try and get in
that door for the next twenty minutes.
So we can pretty much get through this
without any problems. You wronged me
and so I am going to wrong you. All those
useless girls, unemployed, killing their
babies after playing the slut, walking the
earth with no purpose. So I gave them a
purpose. I made them little stars. In the
constellation of the Vain Queen.

ISOBEL   You mutilated who they were.

CHALMERS   But when I made the mistake with that
                  girl, I felt like I had betrayed myself, and
                  her in a way. I had done my work, but then
                  I found the student card in her pocket. I
                  just wanted to hide her. But Isobel, you
                  have made it perfect. Tonight I can finish
                  my project. I can make a pattern. Sarah
                  and Alexandra will always be spoken of
                  together now. Because of you, they lived in
                  the same house, their lives framed by the
                  same walls, looked out the same windows
                  and saw the same things; they took the
                  same bus, they went to the same university.

ISOBEL   Oh Jesus Christ.

ALEXANDRA   Mum?

CHALMERS   I'm not going to kill you, Isobel, not your
                  body. I'm going to make you look at my final
                  pattern and forever see your dead daughter
                  and know that you did it.

ALEXANDRA   Don't kill me.

CHALMERS   Don't be stupid: I've just told you the logic.
                  Of course I'm—

FRANK   (Over a speaker) Alfred. Alfred? Alfred, we
                  can see you. There's nowhere to go with
                  this. Unlock the door and let us in.

CHALMERS   Is that you, Frank?

FRANK   Yes, it's Frank Bowman.

CHALMERS   You going to watch? *(Laughs)* Is Fergus
            there too?

FRANK   No, Fergus is not here.

CHALMERS   That's a pity. How did you turn up?

FRANK   That doesn't matter. What matters—

CHALMERS   You don't fucking tell me what matters,
            that's finished, so you just answer my
            questions now or I start cutting her
            eyes out.

ISOBEL   Frank!

FRANK   Some idiot forgot to tell me your
            'granddaughter' was visiting. Thought it
            didn't matter.

ALEXANDRA   Uncle Frank, he's going to kill me. He said
            he's going to kill me.

FRANK   I won't let that happen.

CHALMERS   You're not in control here, sonny. Bitch is
            dead and a star is born.

JUDITH   The world will see him like the genius he is
            again.

CHALMERS   Shut up, Judith, just watch McArthur.

JUDITH   I shot her in the leg, Alfred, she's not going nowhere.

CHALMERS   Watch her. I don't want you messing this up.

JUDITH   I won't mess it up, I told you I wouldn't.

FRANK   That your real daughter, Chalmers?

CHALMERS   Just a fan, Frank.

ISOBEL   She's a psycho bitch, Frank, she's shot me in the leg.

FRANK   There are people on the way, hang in there.

JUDITH   Who? Who are on the way?

CHALMERS   Shut up and keep your mind on the job.

ISOBEL   If you run now, Judith, you might just make it. A few minutes more and you're ours.

JUDITH   That's not the plan. Can I shoot her, Alfred?

CHALMERS   No!

JUDITH   I shot the fox.

CHALMERS   Don't shoot her!

ALEXANDRA   Mum. Mum, I love you. I'm sorry, Mum. I'm really sorry.

ISOBEL   It's OK, baby. It was all me.

JUDITH   What do I do, Alfred?

CHALMERS Stick to the plan!

JUDITH She's looking at me funny. Stop looking at me, bitch.

ALEXANDRA Mum, stop looking at her!

CHALMERS Isobel, shut up or it starts now.

FRANK Give it up, Chalmers.

ISOBEL You're not him.

JUDITH Then who am I? *(ISOBEL stands up)* Sit down!

CHALMERS Do her other leg.

ISOBEL Get out of here, Judith. Run!

JUDITH I can't.

ISOBEL You can.

JUDITH I can't.

ISOBEL Run, Judith, run.

JUDITH I've nowhere to run to. There's nothing.

She shoots ISOBEL. There's a silence.

FRANK Isobel? Isobel?

ALEXANDRA Mum?

CHALMERS Did you shoot her leg?

JUDITH   No.

CHALMERS   What?

JUDITH   I did it.

CHALMERS   What? Fucking bitch, what?

JUDITH   Right in the heart. She's all gone.

*CHALMERS makes a choice and starts moving towards the
screaming ALEXANDRA.*

FRANK   Alexandra, Alexandra . . . Alex, can you
             hear me?

CHALMERS sits down, disengaged.

CHALMERS   It's dark.

FRANK   Alexandra?

ALEXANDRA   I'm so sorry.

FRANK   Unlock the door . . . let me in.

ALEXANDRA   I want my mum . . . I want my mum . . .
             I love her.

FRANK   It's going to be OK . . . unlock the door.

ALEXANDRA   I love her.

Blackout.

IAN RANKIN and MARK THOMSON

In conversation with the Lyceum's Michelle Mangan

How did Dark Road come about? Who approached who and when did you set about writing the piece?

Ian: I'm fairly sure the original question came from Mark during coffee and chat. Why do we see so many cop shows on TV and so few on the stage? He challenged me to come up with a story that was properly dramatic and meaty. I went away, thought about it, and offered him a few scenarios. He chose the one he felt best suited the stage, and a company of great actors.

Mark: Yes, I definitely was the suitor! And I knew Ian loved the theatre as I often see him at the Lyceum. I think he is one of our great storytellers and I was very intrigued to find a way to get him on our stage in a genre that is celebrated more in novels, TV and film.

Can you give us an insight into the writing process and how you found collaborating together?

Ian: Having storyboarded the play and delineated the main characters, I left it to Mark to write the dialogue. He provided a structure that really worked and we began to bounce ideas, rework dialogue and research back and forth, meeting to go through the script in detail until we had something we could offer actors – roles we felt would challenge and excite them.

Mark: Ian story, me dialogue, allowed us to get to know and trust each other. But there is Rankin dialogue in the play as well as plot developments that emerged once I started to write the dialogue. We spent a great deal of time tuning into each other. For example (I'll mention the R word here), we did talk about Rebus but quickly dismissed it as a predictable choice – he already exists both on the page and screen. I think we were clear that constructing a story from scratch, that would be best told on stage, was our ambition.

When it came to casting, did you both have a say in that?

Ian: From the word go, Mark had Maureen Beattie in mind and I left the casting decisions to him – he is the expert, after all! But I've been thrilled by the way rehearsals have gone, the ensemble spark off each other in ways I hadn't imagined.

Mark: Yes, ultimately it's the director's job to cast but I always ask playwrights' views. Is there anyone comes into their head? We bounced ideas about, mostly to come to some sense of the kind of animal we were looking for. Then I got on with it. And now we have a room that is a lively mix of great experience and terrific young talent, all united in intelligence and generosity.

Ian, how have you found the experience of writing for the stage and how did you feel in the rehearsal room watching your characters come to life?

Ian: The initial few days of read-throughs were interesting in themselves, but when we moved to rehearsals it got even better. Seeing the stage design was an amazing moment, too. It really is very special and solved some problems we had with the structure of the piece. Never having been in a theatre workshop environment, it's been a real privilege to see the actors begin to inhabit their roles. I've been put on the spot a few times, too. The characters in my books don't often turn to me and say 'I'm not really sure what's happening here'! Or there will be a query about procedure. One headache has been the reorganisation of Police Scotland – the play was written before the changes that took place in April 2013. Maureen's character has gone from being a chief constable (in the original draft) to a chief superintendent – as a direct result of the reorganisation.

Tell us a bit about the main themes of the play and give us an insight into your characters.

Ian: It's a psychodrama, I suppose, but also very firmly about family – the family you have at home, and the family your colleagues become when you join the police force. Isobel begins to wonder what she has lost as a result of climbing the greasy pole, and also suspects that her whole career has been constructed from a lie. I'd happily give more away than that, but Mark would probably kill me . . .

Mark: Yes, we don't want any famous writers being bumped off, that would be a terrible shame! I think Ian's highlighted the world of the play and I think our relationship with our own past is very strong in it, too. What was so vivid and inspiring was Ian's creation of the protagonists. Even the names resonated immediately. I mean, 'Black Fergus'! Who else but Ian could create him? You just know there's this creature hewn from the grey, unyielding Calvinist walls of our most austere churches.

Any stories you want to share from the rehearsal room?

Ian: Having spent a week and a bit in rehearsal, I then had to head off to Cape Town, so Mark probably has more stories than I do. But as someone who has often visited the theatre, but never been allowed behind the scenes until now, I've been fascinated by the stuff I've not been aware of, such as how to make entrances and exits. The actors will ask, 'Is this door going to open inwards or outwards?' And they need to know, of course. There is a real sense of detailed choreography and if that occasionally goes wrong in rehearsal, it allows for some laughter.

Mark: What happens in rehearsals stays in rehearsals! I suppose one thing I would say is that when you're doing something that has a real nastiness, real emotional pain and horror, then it's important to keep laughter high. You can't just stare and stare at the awfulness or you'll lose perspective.

As rehearsals have progressed, have you discovered any new elements in the play that weren't in your original vision?

Mark: Not new elements, no, but the journey of rehearsals can often mean that a scene has something under it that you didn't realise. The biggest thing in doing a crime piece is that we must make sure it adds up. Ambiguity and doubt are vital to the pleasure of seeing something like this, but it must be precise. And also the actors must keep their integrity always and never just play something because it helps create a useful doubt. Every action and thing that's said must come from somewhere real and honest.

Has the play changed during the rehearsal process?

Ian: While I was in South Africa, Mark sent me an email saying: 'No biggie, but I've just changed the order of a couple of scenes.' He explained the reasoning and I agreed with his decision. The actors are also chipping in, suggesting changes in phrasing to match their characters' personalities, or finding humour, by use of a facial expression or gesture, that elevates a moment in a scene.

Mark: I think what Ian mentions was the most significant – a little restructuring in the first half. The rest has been about cutting and fine-tuning rather than overhaul. However, the journey with how you play a scene may well shift quite radically. What you thought might work turns out to give the game away. So we all make character choices that help us construct this – what Barrie Keeffe called 'a pyramid of cards' – where if one card is out of place the whole bloody pack could come crumbling down. So we're placing them carefully!

Would you both do it again?

Ian: Would I write for the theatre again? Ask me when the Edinburgh run has ended!

Mark: Well, I've loved the process with Ian. He's been amazingly cool about entering this very collaborative world. As he says, as a novelist he sits in front of his computer and what he says goes, right from the story choices to whether the sun is out, or a character cries, is staring at another or sitting in a chair. Now he's thrown in with all of us collaborating over everything. Not one storm-out! Quite the opposite, in fact. I think he got the bug and enjoyed the buzz of having a set of sparky creative people in a room, hell-bent on finding the best way to tell his story.

THE CONVERSATION CONTINUES

Ian Rankin and Mark Thomson on *Dark Road*

Ian: Mark, my memory is that *Dark Road* started life almost as a dare – the question being: would a contemporary cop drama work on stage? Is that how you remember it?

Mark: Yes. I think it really started when you did a talk at the Lyceum on my production of James Hogg's *Confessions of a Justified Sinner*. I'd say we first bonded over literature and one of the greatest crime novels ever written. But then a few lunches later I remember us wondering how the crime genre might work on stage. I mean, I know there are Agatha Christies, but how possible was it to satisfy the fun and tension of a modern crime novel such as Ian's? Then the dare . . .

Ian: When I first pitched the plot to you, I think the central character was male. But you had a particular actor in mind, and asked if we could have a woman chief of police instead – and that totally changed the dynamic! Fortuitously so, I now think! Do you agree?

Mark: Yes, I remember that. Strange, because of course now you can't imagine it being a man. It's absolutely the story of an extraordinary woman in extraordinary circumstances. I did think, too, that getting away from Rebus would be healthy and interesting for you. A new adventure! And yes, I definitely suggested that there were a number of very strong Scottish actresses that would reward the piece, namely Maureen.

Ian: How would you describe the play? I've found myself calling it a drama of mind games and sexual politics. There is a whodunit element, too, of course . . .

Mark: I absolutely agree with that. I remember us talking about the tone and content. It had to celebrate your voice on stage. People were going to come and they would want to see your dark stories with vivid characters, twists and tensions. But OK, how would I describe our play? I think it's the story of a woman at a critical point in her life, needing to revisit the past before she can move, in any sense, to her future. The play is about the difficulties of finding truth in the past because you're not there. You're here and now. It's also the story of a mother and daughter.

Ian: Writing a play is one thing, but getting it ready for the stage is quite another matter. How traumatic was that?

Mark: Well, without sounding melodramatic, I always feel like it is a real cocktail of pragmatism and intense creativity. Every choice – whether it's casting, set, composer – starts to define and determine what the evening can be. It's full of fear and excitement. But I like all that. Who wants to do anything you don't care enough about to fear its failure?

Ian: After the first preview, you made a couple of big decisions, cutting one scene and lessening the body count at the end. As a newbie, it amazes me that this is possible – and that all those changes worked!

Mark: I think they did, Ian. It's the most I think I have ever changed over previews. But that was about us figuring out what worked and what didn't work regarding the crime drama. I remember needing more whisky than Rebus when I got home every night! But what was terrific and very lucky is that I always felt we travelled together. When things don't work and you have co-authors, then that can be tricky.

Ian: It seems to me that the set design solved quite a few potential problems, by being flexible as well as completely stunning. How important is it to you that theatre be immersive?

Mark: Entirely. I always say that the evening has to take the audience on a journey that is unpredictable and interesting. And the set had to do quite a lot of that work. Francis O'Connor is brilliant at taking care of how to find a physical articulation of story and create pleasing acrobatic solutions to whatever a play throws at him. We needed people to get lost in our dark world and not let them out till the house lights went up. The set, and of course the lights and music, all drew people in and sustained that tension.

Ian: Of course, with such complex staging, there must have been many potential pitfalls. Did you have any problems with it?

Mark: Well, the set was a revolve that had the three different locations on it. In the centre of it was a kind of weirdly shaped mini-room where most of the quick changes took place. During one show, poor Maureen was changing in one corner of it. But it was the wrong corner. Jo, our dresser, suddenly realised there was a wee section of the audience enjoying a view of Maureen in a state of undress that was definitely not required in the play, and had to howk her away.

Ian: The audiences were huge – I struggled to get a ticket some nights! And many of those people hardly ever went to the theatre. So do you think we proved our point with *Dark Road*?

Mark: Yes, we did. We made people jump. We entertained them. We kept them guessing. And the bar sales tell me that once we'd had our way with them, they needed a good bloody drink. I'm happy with that.

BEHIND THE SCENES

with Jo Rush
Assistant director at the Royal Lyceum Theatre Edinburgh

In the run-up to *Dark Road*'s opening night, assistant director Jo Rush kept a weekly rehearsal-room diary charting the play's journey from page to stage . . .

August 26th 2013
Today is the day that rehearsals for *Dark Road* officially begin.

I have personally been excited for this day since March and now that it's finally here I can't quite believe it.

Over the last five months, since I became assistant director to Mark Thomson, who has co-written this play with Ian Rankin, there has already been a huge amount to do before reaching this stage where at last we have actors, scripts and production team all in one rehearsal room together.

As an assistant director, my role is to support Mark's direction and provide a second opinion and sounding board for his ideas at all stages of the production, which gives me an amazing insight into how the play is put together.

As Mark has also written the script, an extra perspective is really helpful. In the build-up to starting rehearsals my role has entailed script reading, research, design meetings, casting, photo shoots and a surprising amount of secrecy.

Dark Road will be a world premiere for the Lyceum and the first time that Ian Rankin has written for the stage, so when I first found out that I would be working on the production I couldn't even tell anyone what the play was as it hadn't yet been formally announced.

And even now that the play is out in the public eye, the nature of the piece demands a certain level of caution when discussing it. Unlike many productions of classic plays with well-known plots, *Dark Road* is entirely new and needs to remain a complete surprise for the audience so they can best feel its impact. I would hate to deprive anyone of the feeling of exhilaration and confusion I had when I first hurtled to the conclusion of the play, so I'm being very careful not to give any spoilers!

I've worked with new writing previously at the Traverse where I have been an assistant director to Orla O'Loughlin and also directed at their Words, Words, Words new playwriting events so by now I'm used to reading various drafts of scripts with an eye out for confusions and inconsistencies and making sure the script flows.

For this collaboration, Ian has created the characters and content of the play and Mark has provided its dramatic shape and it is fascinating to see how enmeshed their writing has become. The play has a distinct, familiar Rankin flavour that sits perfectly within Mark's great ability to build drama and pace.

What makes Ian's work so recognisable and so perfect for the Lyceum is the way it is embedded in the geography of Scotland and particularly of Edinburgh. The familiarity of local monuments and street names is disrupted and disturbed by the crime scenes and bodies that his writing confronts you with.

I've enjoyed watching as these details become clearer in each draft of the script and couldn't quite stop myself shuddering uneasily as I read the latest draft and realised one of the murder victims lived just around the corner from me.

The work done in the last few months has given a series of teasing tastes of what this production will become. I've been able to see how the world of the play will look on stage by attending design meetings where the whole stage is shrunk to model size by the designer before being built for real by the Lyceum team at Roseburn.

I've spent the day worrying tourists and locals as we took photos of 'murder victims' in locations around the city to create crime-scene images – it seems only one person called the police on us! In casting meetings I've heard accomplished actors reading sections of the text and been given a tantalising glimpse of its potential.

And I've learnt far more than I ever expected to know about secure unit hospitals and police interview tape recorders.

But now, on day one of rehearsals, it's as simple as: one rehearsal room, eight actors, one director, one stage manager, one amazing script – and me.

And I can't wait to see it come to life.

September 3rd 2013

Getting to know you: Week one on the Royal Lyceum's *Dark Road*

After the months of waiting, somehow the first week of rehearsals for *Dark Road* has already sped by and it's suddenly September already.

We've had a brilliant week of getting to know each other and getting to grips with the complexities of the script. And it all began with day one and our first impressions.

You can never recreate a first impression. When working with a script the first reaction you have on reading it is often the closest you can get to what the audience will eventually experience so it's really important to pay attention to these impressions and ideas before becoming too familiar with the play.

Ian Rankin, Jo Rush and Mark Thomson during rehearsals.
Photo © Dan Travis, Deputy Stage Manager, Royal Lyceum Theatre

We spent the first day and a half of our rehearsals going through the play scene by scene and seeing what questions were raised at the end of each scene. This was really valuable time for all of us as the crime thriller genre demands a clarity of storyline and plotting that we had to ensure made sense.

We were lucky enough to have Ian Rankin present in rehearsals with us for the whole of last week before he jetted off to a book festival in South Africa. Ian has been a great help whenever clarification of the story has been needed, particularly of unseen or secret parts of the plot that never appear on stage. And it's been really enjoyable to get an insight into his first impressions of rehearsing a stage play; being surprised by how many questions the actors asked and the different storytelling tools available in plays compared to novels.

> 'There's all these internal things going on that you can write in a novel but you don't have them on stage'
>
> Ian Rankin

Ian and I have both been figuring out the best way to contribute in the rehearsal room. As assistant director there is no hard and fast rule to define my role in the rehearsal process; I'm there to support the director in whatever way is needed, which necessarily changes depending on the director you're working with. Ian, as a co-writer, and especially one who is working so closely with the play's director, is in a similar position.

Some writers are never in rehearsal, others choose to be there all day, every day, and involved in every decision about the play. Ian has been striking a great balance between the two: finding the right time to give rewrites, not interrupting the flow of rehearsals, but there to provide help and clarity when needed. As a result, the cast have felt really encouraged by his supportive attitude and 'benevolent presence' in the room and have felt able to voice any questions they have, which is key to the next phase of rehearsals we entered into.

Asking the right questions – actually, just asking any questions, no matter how silly they may sometimes sound – is vital in the first week of rehearsals. You have to throw ideas around and play with a lot of different possible meanings without landing on answers at this early stage. It's as simple as just trying stuff out and using a process of elimination – every idea you reject gets you closer to the right answer.

> 'Can you do it like Dennis Hopper in *Apocalypse Now*?'
> Mark Thomson (to young *female* actor)

Because of this, lots of suggestions get thrown out there that are designed to help the actors explore what subtext is underlying each scene and from that point to see how much it's actually possible to play.

You may decide that a character has a chronic fear of light switches due to an electric shock received at their third birthday party but can you play that without having to just tell the audience? Or do you just show that they never switch on the lights? Sometimes actually all you can play is what's written, what the characters say or do. But you have to ask questions first before you can know this for sure.

One of the more hilarious suggestions we encountered this week was whether or not our heroine would have a 'vajazzle' – we quickly decided that of course she wouldn't – but not before an awkward conversation where the exact definition of a vajazzle had to be explained to Mark . . . !

As we progressed through the first week and became more in tune with the play and its characters we found that the answers to our questions came more easily, but there is still a lot of exploration to be done. The richness and intrigue of this play lies in its complex characters and their relationships with one another and the fact that sometimes their actions are confusing even to themselves and can't be rationalised by us or by an audience, they simply act first and think later. And all of that is part of the story we have to tell.

Educating Ian:

Ian – 'It's funny how she mentions her three hundred and sixty-three followers on Twitter.'

Me – 'But that's because to us mere mortals that's actually loads! We can't all have sixty-two thousand followers!'

September 9th, 2013

Learning the walk: Week two on the Royal Lyceum's *Dark Road*

Getting the show on its feet so that the characters move and inhabit the world of the play has been the next stage of our rehearsal process for *Dark Road*.

It sounds so simple. Step 1: actor delivers line; step 2: actor moves around stage; step 3: actor combines moving and speaking *at same time* – and there you have a fully realised stage production!

But thankfully it is far from being this straightforward and the kind of stilted productions caused by this oversimplified attitude towards staging are a rare mistake.

Just as we have subjected the script to intense questioning and played with the options available to us, we have also approached the movement of the characters in this manner.

> Anonymous actor – 'You know when you start questioning yourself and you forget how to walk?'

You have to examine the impulses and energy of each character to find the way in which they should move in the stage space, asking the easy questions of 'Where do they need to be and when?' and also the more complex questions of motivations and reactions: 'How do they respond physically to other people?'; 'How comfortable do they feel in this particular setting?'

Rather than fix on set movements from A to B at this stage in rehearsal, Mark has encouraged the cast to move freely within the space in order to find what works and what doesn't. Although some decisions – such as which door a character enters through – need to be made to make sense of a scene, on the whole, it's not helpful to get weighed down in staging movement too early.

If you do so, it can drain the playfulness and energy of a rehearsal and prevent the actors from fully exploring the dynamic and meaning of a scene because they are focused on where they need to move, when.

Walking and talking at the same time may sound fairly uncomplicated, but when you're asking an actor to speak and to move in a psychologically believable way for the character that they are playing, you are asking a huge amount of them and it's easy to over-think this, which is why it's best not to get bogged down in it while

Walking the walk in the rehearsal room.
Photo © Dan Travis, Deputy Stage Manager, Royal Lyceum Theatre

vital work on the heart of the story and characters is still ongoing.

In my role as assistant director, one of the ways that I have been best able to contribute to the production has been in creating a precise timeline for the play's events. To do this I sat down with the script and went over it in detail for any reference to when events happen, how much time passes between one scene and the next, and what events happen in between scenes that we don't see on stage.

As the play takes place over several months in 2013 but also includes events that occurred in 1988, it can be difficult to keep track of the order of events. For the actors this is crucial as they need to understand what their character has experienced and knows at each point in the play to inform their character decisions for each scene.

The actors have to forget the full context and storyline of the play that they are aware of as actors and only respond to what their character knows at any given point so they are able to create a truthful reaction to the events their character experiences.

Being given definitive control over the play timeline has let out all my worst pedantic tendencies, earning me the nickname 'Timeline Fascist'. But having a very specific timeline is also so useful in making sure that all elements of our plot make sense and for the design team who can change clothes and lighting according to the time of year it is in the play. For me, it gives me a real feeling of connection with the events of the play and an understanding of it. Tomorrow morning, my timeline is going up on the rehearsal room wall for all the company to see and, despite the unfortunate dictator-associated nickname, I (not-so-secretly) love being a 'Timeline Fascist'!

September 16th 2013

Dark comedy: Week three on the Royal Lyceum's *Dark Road*

It's fair to say that Ian Rankin and Mark Thomson's first play together is not exactly a light-hearted farce – many apologies to anyone whose expectations have now been shattered. And yet the presiding theme of our third week of rehearsals has been laughter.

Maybe it's the pressure from the ever-approaching deadline of first night, or perhaps it's the tension that builds up when you're rehearsing intense, dramatic scenes simply finding a way to be released. Either way, it's always the most serious scenes that are creating the most hilarity – with the steeliest of actors and directors reduced to fits of giggles by a surly-sounding secretary or an unyielding prop.

There are several benefits to a rehearsal room full of laughter, besides the obvious fact that it's a lot of fun. A company that are having a laugh and sharing in-jokes with each other is usually a well-bonded company. When you're spending so much time together it's a blessing if you can enjoy joking around and it boosts the morale and trust of the team, especially as you develop jokes that are personal to the show.

A particular source of entertainment in the company comes from suggestions of what would feature in *Dark Road: The Musical* with actors (and even our director) sometimes unable to resist the temptation to burst into a song and dance.

In a strange way, as you rehearse through each scene of the play it's really good for the actors to get any accidental funny moments out of their system so that they don't get thrown by them at a later date and end up dissolving with laughter mid-performance.

The particular challenge that we've been facing in *Dark Road* is how to allow for select moments of humour within the play but avoid unintentional humour at all

Director Mark Thomson in musical theatre mode.
Photo © Dan Travis, Deputy Stage Manager, Royal Lyceum Theatre

costs. The last thing that anyone wants is a moment or phrase that seems too clichéd, innuendo-laden, or silly and raises a titter from the audience that destroys the drama of a scene. So we have to watch out along the way and flag up anything that might illicit an undesirable audience-chuckle.

Now that we're fully into the process of finalising the play's shape, seeing how each scene will look and what movements and moments will tell the story best, we are also adding in more props and costume to rehearsals. This is exciting as it fleshes out the look of the play, bringing us closer to seeing what its final appearance will be like.

Props are often not an actor's best friend. It may seem simple to open a cassette player, place a tape inside and press play. But, under the pressure of a performance and with lines, movements and timing to remember, it's surprising how easily those things can go wrong. Through practising the movements and action of each scene and using props as repetitively as possible throughout the rehearsal process the cast can build up their muscle-memory which will allow them to move without having to think about it and result in an action that appears natural in performance.

With more props in the room comes more opportunity for hilarity and (temporary) confusion. The cast have particularly enjoyed spinning round and round on the egg chair that features in the set, berating an imaginary secretary via telephone handset, and discussing how best to achieve a grotesque-looking eyeball. And our sincere hope is that all of the many things that could go wrong with props go wrong now in rehearsal rather than during the run . . .

Two of our cast members, Maureen Beattie and Phil Whitchurch, have already been experiencing show-related nightmares, which at present mostly centre on the horror of finding yourself in the middle of a scene with no idea of what the lines are or even what the scene is.

I was initiated into the nightmare-club myself on Friday last week when I dreamt that, having missed a day of rehearsals, I came back to find that the entire story had been relocated to America and turned into a cheap melodrama (complete with a tearful pregnant woman arriving on someone's doorstep in the pouring rain – I've no idea who she was!).

I woke up absolutely raging that the exciting, Edinburgh-based play I'd waited so long to see come to life would never be put on the stage. You can imagine the relief I felt when I realised that it was all in my imagination.

Company illness of the week:
Metaphor fatigue – the loss of ability to express anything via an appropriate verbal metaphor, symptomatic of end-of-week-three-itis and evidenced by a string of unrelated nouns and verbs jumbled together and ended with a sigh. E.g. 'when there's – but you're reaching – for the thing – the goal – and you still gather the cake.'

September 24th, 2013

Staggering through: Week four on the Royal Lyceum's *Dark Road*

The fourth week of rehearsals for *Dark Road* has seen us make the biggest transition of our rehearsal process so far – out of the rehearsal room and into the theatre. Hopefully the experience won't prove as traumatic as the proverb that phrase is riffing on!

Having spent four weeks in the rehearsal room – which is over the road from the theatre itself – we had all become comfortable in that familiar environment and the theatre space had started to feel strangely distant, to me at least. But with the beginning of week four reality hit with a bump – the set was not only fully built but already being assembled in the theatre and the Lyceum's excellent team of lighting, sound and technical crew were preparing for our arrival. Were we ready?

On Monday, while still in the rehearsal room, we attempted our first 'stagger through'. This is a fairly self-descriptive name used for the first time you run the play all the way through from beginning to end. Whereas you might call this a full 'run' of the play, describing it as a 'stagger' shows an awareness that everyone is doing this for the first time and are unlikely to be able to run before they can walk.

For the cast it is a particularly interesting experience to put all the scenes in order for the first time and see what stories are being told in the scenes that they don't appear in and how different plot lines sit next to each other in the body of the play. On the technical side, it was an opportunity for our lighting designer, Malcolm, to see the shape of the play, to see where the actors are moving and how they're using the set so that he can plan how best to light the show and get as many of those lights set up in the theatre ahead of our arrival.

Stage management, wardrobe, and our designer Francis also watched the stagger-through with a view to where changes could be made and how to plan for the smoothest possible working of the final show. It's safe to say there was a high level of concentration in the room which, when combined with the tense nature of the play, left us completely wiped out afterwards.

Working on a brand new play usually means that adjustments are being made to the script until very late in the process. Previous new plays that I've worked on have even been subject to rewrites after their first previews! Keeping track of the many changes to the script along the way and making sure that a master copy of the script is kept up to date has been one of the tasks that myself and Dan, our wonderful deputy stage manager, have been grappling with on a daily basis. It's so important to have a record of all the changes to the text because this will be the reference point for all the complicated cueing of lights, sound, and everything else so it needs to be as accurate as possible.

Bizarre moment of the week: having returned to us from South Africa, Ian – ever the most culturally savvy in the room – seemed to particularly enjoy explaining to two younger members of the company what 'twerking' is!

After Monday's stagger-through Mark went away and

made some cuts to the script to ensure that it would run at a good length on the stage and so on Tuesday we had to quickly take on these cuts and work with the actors whose lines were affected to get them used to the edits. Although it's occasionally sad when the play loses a particular phrase you've grown attached to, most of the cuts have simply helped us to avoid saying the same thing twice, or introducing information tangents that aren't needed in a scene, so the play now flows even better as a result.

After this, the bulk of our fourth week was all about repetition, repetition, repetition. Going over scenes again and again to get them built into the cast's muscle-memory and giving extra time to scenes or sections that caused difficulties to the actors so that they could overcome any problems and hone the scene through consistent practice.

By lunchtime on Friday we were ready to run! We had a proper full run of the show that afternoon in the rehearsal room with the whole production team watching and the difference that those four days had made was remarkable. With that done there was only one thing left to do – pack up our props and set and move into the theatre.

And that's where we've been for the last few days. Getting used to our new home, trying to understand the intricacies of the set, seeing costume, set, lighting and sound all finally come together. There's a lot that is still to be figured out before opening night but it's going to be amazing to see it get there through this final push.

September 25th, 2013

All tech-ed up: The final week on the Royal Lyceum's *Dark Road*

The final week leading up to our official opening night of *Dark Road* has been surreal to say the least. During tech week everyone essentially lives at the theatre all day, every day.

You start to lose touch with the outside world – and find it hard to explain to any friends who manage to make contact with you why you are so sleep-deprived and oversensitive!

The job of tech week is to bring together the full technical elements of the show: set, lighting, sound, projection and costume, with the work the actors have already created in the rehearsal room – and then to make the full effect as polished as possible.

Technical rehearsals can be very stop-and-start because if a cue doesn't go right you have to pause and correct the problem. So you rarely get to run a scene from beginning to end without stopping, never mind the whole play.

We are working with a revolve set which allows us to swap between several locations on stage without long, full changes of set between each scene. Being able to move quickly from one location to another is vital for this play as it helps us to build momentum and pace and keep the action of the play moving forward.

However, it also throws up many difficulties. Our set has been amazingly designed to provide three different locations, but as a result when actors are exiting a scene they have to be extremely careful that they don't walk

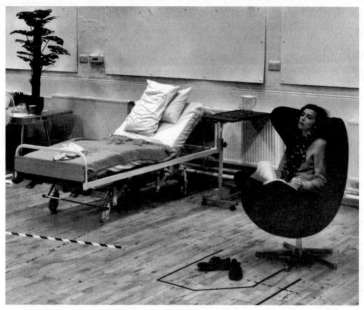

Sarah Vickers at home in the rehearsal room.
Photo © Dan Travis, Deputy Stage Manager, Royal Lyceum Theatre

straight into the next scene. And when you're stood at the centre of a revolving set of doors it can be very hard to remember which door will lead you safely offstage and which will accidentally reveal you to the entire audience! This has led to much confusion and hilarity backstage with one actor often heard saying, 'I don't know where I am or where I'm going!'

A lot of our time during tech week has been spent working out how to perfect transitions between scenes. It is not just about the actors finally putting their performances onto the stage but also about the backstage crew being given time to rehearse their roles in making the play happen.

The stage management team have the tricky task of making sure each scene is set correctly, with all the right props and furnishings, without ever being seen onstage themselves as that would break the illusion of the world we are trying to create.

Due to the fast pace of the show there are also a number of lightning-quick wardrobe changes that the actors have to make. Sometimes with less than a minute between leaving a scene and appearing in the next scene in a totally different outfit.

Zoe and Jo, our assistant stage manager and dresser, spend most of the show hiding in various tiny corners of the revolve making sure that all this can happen, and occasionally having to push actors out of view of the audience when a door swings open at the wrong time. It's a mind-bending task that they're faced with and the show just wouldn't be able to work without them.

My role during tech week has mostly involved running up and down the three floors of the theatre's auditorium to check sight lines and ensure that all the action onstage can be seen and heard by the full audience – all 658 seats!

I've also been running lines with the actors whenever they're not needed onstage, standing in for them while lights and sound are plotted during breaks, and taking note of scenes we want to work on and feeding back ideas to the cast.

September 28th 2013

Previews: The last few steps on the Royal Lyceum's *Dark Road*

Previews are like the laboratory trial for a show. In a preview you recreate the conditions of the final production as closely as possible by having all the technical elements of the play in place and putting it in front of an audience.

And, just like in a dress rehearsal, it's important to note things that are working and things that aren't so you can address them the next day.

Ian Rankin

Photo © Dan Travis, Deputy Stage Manager, Royal Lyceum Theatre

But a preview is not the finished article. You need the previews to teach you how an audience reacts to the play and what technical problems might occur so that you can then refine the production accordingly.

We have been lucky to have three preview performances before tonight's official opening and this has taught us so much.

On Wednesday, when we found that the finale of the play that had worked so well in the rehearsal room just wasn't getting the desired response from the audience, we were able to change it.

On Thursday we trialled our new ending and found it much better but still in need of tweaking.

And last night, on Friday, we were able to present a slightly altered version of our new ending that we are really happy with and the audience really responded to.

We've also cut scenes and reordered the play over the previews and this has been essential in giving us a play that tells the story we want the audience to see and takes them on the right kind of journey. Without previews we wouldn't have had the flexibility to change these things or the audience feedback to know what needed changing.

I've really enjoyed seeing how different audiences react to the show, and gathering feedback in the interval and at the end to see what people predict will happen and how satisfied they were with the story. The most gratifying thing of all has been watching from the back of the stalls as people jump out of their seats and scream and gasp in all the right places so we know we've hit the thriller mark.

Tonight's opening night will be a much needed chance to put on nice clothes and socialise after all the madness and changes of this week. But it's been totally worth it because we now have a show that we are all really proud of and excited to share, so all there is left to do is officially open it to the public!

Photo © Dan Travis, Deputy Stage Manager, Royal Lyceum Theatre